THE GLIMMERING GHOST

A strange noise, echoing through the treetops, woke Linda. She waited for the sound to come again, but the night was suddenly quiet. A spooky kind of quiet.

Linda shook her head. "You must have been dreaming," she told herself.

Ta-thump. Ta-thump. Thump, thump. There it was again—the sound of a horse galloping. Linda unzipped her sleeping bag, then silently tiptoed away from the campground. She found Amber pawing the ground nervously.

"Did you hear it too, girl?" she asked the mare.

Amber pricked up her ears and stared at the top of the mountain. Linda followed the horse's gaze. Then she saw it, and her pulse began to race.

Ta-thump. Ta-thump. A coal black horse, just like the Ghost Horse, was galloping along the rocky ridge!

Books in The Linda Craig Adventure series:

#1 The Golden Secret
#2 A Star for Linda
#3 The Silver Stallion
#4 The Crystal Trail
#5 The Glimmering Ghost

Available from MINSTREL Books

THE GLIMMERING GHOST

By Ann Sheldon

PUBLISHED BY POCKET BOOKS

New York London Toronto Sydney Tokyo

This novel is a work of fiction. Names, characters, places and incidents are either the product of the author's imagination or are used fictitiously. Any resemblance to actual events or locales or persons, living or dead, is entirely coincidental.

A MINSTREL PAPERBACK *ORIGINAL*

A Minstrel Book published by
POCKET BOOKS, a division of Simon & Schuster Inc.
1230 Avenue of the Americas, New York, NY 10020

Produced by Mega-Books of New York, Inc.

ISBN: 0-671-64038-0

First Minstrel Books printing January 1989

10 9 8 7 6 5 4 3 2 1

Printed in the U.S.A.

1 ♦♦♦♦

"Hey, Amber! Quit fooling around," twelve-year-old Linda Craig said as her palomino mare snatched the yellow- and blue-striped saddle blanket between her teeth.

Amber tossed her golden head, and the blanket flapped in the air.

Linda was used to Amber's tricks and didn't usually mind the mare's playfulness. But this afternoon she was in a hurry. Linda, her brother Bob, and their friends Larry Spencer and Kathy Hamilton were going on an overnight ride to Coyote Mountain. They were going to help Mac, the ranch foreman, round up some stray cattle. Bob and Mac had already saddled their horses. Larry and Kathy would be arriving at Rancho del Sol any minute.

"Come on, girl." Linda tried to make her voice sound stern. "Give it back. We have to get going!"

Amber dropped the blanket into Linda's hand as if she understood, then nuzzled Linda's shoulder with her nose.

"We'll play later," Linda said as she swung the blanket, then the saddle, onto Amber's back.

"Hey, slowpoke, what's taking you so long?" Bob Craig, Linda's fifteen-year-old brother, leaned over the stall door. His cowboy hat was tilted back on his head, and a lock of sandy blond hair peeked from beneath the brim. "Is Amber up to her usual tricks?"

Linda secured the saddle. "Nothing I can't handle," she replied as she tightened the girth by pulling on the strap circling Amber's body. She didn't want her older brother to think she couldn't control her frisky mare. "Amber was just feeling playful," she added, reaching into her pocket for a piece of carrot. She offered it to Amber with a flat palm. The mare took it daintily.

"Okay, we're just about ready to go," Linda said as she smoothed her long, dark hair into a ponytail and tucked it under her cowboy hat.

"Don't forget your bedroll," Bob said, handing it to her over the door. "You'll need it."

Linda laughed. "Don't worry," she said as she took the bedroll from him. "I don't intend to sleep on cold, rocky ground—not directly, that is." She was tying the bedroll to the back of Amber's saddle when a loud "Yahoo!" and the sound of galloping hooves made her look up.

"Must be Larry." Bob chuckled as he turned and headed toward the barn door to meet his best friend.

Linda waited for Amber to finish chewing the carrot. Then she slipped the bit of the bridle into the mare's mouth and slid the headstall over Amber's ears. As Linda smoothed the mare's long, white forelock, Amber nuzzled her pockets, searching for another treat.

"No more today, girl. We've got to get going," Linda said. She pushed open the stall door and led the palomino down the aisle.

"Morning!" A husky voice greeted them from one of the stalls.

Linda halted Amber and peered over the stall door. Mac was tying sacks of feed for the horses onto the back of a packhorse named Freeloader. Linda grinned. Freeloader already had a large pot and several other sacks dangling from his sturdy body. But since they'd be camping overnight in the mountains, they'd need lots of supplies.

"Glad I'm not the last one ready," Linda said, her brown eyes twinkling.

Mac chuckled and backed Freeloader into the aisle. Then he and Linda led the horses outside into the beautiful Southern California afternoon.

For a second, Linda blinked in the bright sunlight. Then she saw Kathy Hamilton, her best friend, riding up on her pinto horse, Patches. Linda waved.

Kathy waved back, a huge smile on her round freckled face. "Hi!" she called out excitedly. "Is everyone ready?"

"You bet!" a voice answered, and a moment later the girls saw Larry Spencer, mounted on his Appaloosa, Snowbird, come galloping full speed from behind the barn.

"Hey! Slow down!" Linda yelled.

Larry pulled his horse to a halt by the barn door, then made Snowbird rear up on his hind legs. "Yee-ya!" He waved his hat over his head.

"Larry Spencer, you'd better cut that out before someone gets hurt!" Kathy scolded.

"Hey, take it easy." Larry plopped his hat on his head. "I'm just having a little fun."

With that, he made Snowbird rear up again. Only this time, as the Appaloosa began lashing the air with his hooves, Larry lost his balance and slid out of the saddle.

"Ouch!" he yelped as he landed on the ground in a cloud of dust.

For a moment Larry lay motionless. Then he sprang to his feet and began brushing himself off.

"Serves you right," Mac said, untying Buck from the corral fence. He had left his buckskin quarter horse tethered there when he went to get Freeloader.

"You can say that again," Kathy said, laughing. "I think the big show-off got exactly what he deserved."

"It looks like Snowbird thinks so, too." Linda giggled, watching the Appaloosa dodge Larry's attempt to grab hold of his reins.

"Well, no sense in all of us losing what's left of the day," Mac said. "The boys can catch up to us. I want to make camp in plenty of time to give the horses a good rest. Tomorrow we'll have to be up early to look for those strays."

Motioning Buck forward, Mac nodded to the girls to follow. Linda urged Amber into a walk, and the three riders passed the corral toward the rugged foothills that would eventually lead them up into the distant mountain range.

The four-hour trip across the mesa, sparsely covered by prickly totem pole cacti and desert bushes, had been hot, dusty, and dry. But now that they were almost to the top of Coyote Mountain, the scenery had changed.

As the riders wound their way up an old miner's trail, they passed tall ponderosa pines and majestic firs. A flock of bluebirds flew overhead, and a dusky grouse whirred into the bushes.

"It's really beautiful up here!" Kathy called ahead to Linda. The group was riding single file, and Kathy and Patches were right behind Linda and Amber.

"It sure is, but trying to catch up with you guys has made me hungry!" Bob called before Linda could answer. "I hope we make camp soon." He leaned over and gave his bay gelding, Rocket, a pat on the neck. "Rocket could use some dinner, too!"

A few minutes later, as if in answer to Bob's words, Mac rode Buck off the trail and into a grassy clearing. They were about a hundred yards below the highest peak of the mountain.

"We'll camp here," Mac said, halting his horse. "Everyone knows their job, so let's get to work!"

Linda jumped off Amber and led her to a flat area in a grove of pines at the edge of a campsite. She and Kathy were responsible for the horses, so they set to work unsaddling and feeding them. By the time they'd finished, the boys had built a roaring fire, and Mac was stirring something in a big pot.

"Pork and beans, my uncle Harry's secret recipe," Mac said as he dished them each a heaping plateful.

"I hope it's hot," Linda said. "I need something to warm me up!" She took her plate, then sat on a log beside the fire, huddling next to the crackling flames.

"It always cools off in the mountains at night," Mac told her. "Even in the summer."

Linda nodded. Here it was July, yet as soon as the sun disappeared behind the rocky mountaintop, the air had grown chilly.

"Good grub!" Larry told Mac as he polished off the last bit on his plate. "Is there enough left over for seconds?"

Bob held out his plate, too. "You sure this is your uncle's secret recipe?" he asked Mac.

"Sure is!" Mac replied.

"Then what's this?" Bob held up an empty can. The label read "Old West Pork and Beans."

When they all saw the label, they burst out laughing, including Mac.

"I never said it was original, just secret."

"Oh, Mac," Kathy exclaimed. "I'll bet you don't even have an uncle Harry."

"How did you guess?" Mac said, his leathery face breaking into a grin.

"That's easy. We all know you're a storyteller," Linda said.

"Yeah, when Linda and I were kids, Mac used to tell us stories all the time," Bob added.

"Ghost stories!" Linda said in a spooky voice.

"Oooh! Tell us one now!" Kathy cried.

Mac stood up and stretched. "Okay. How about

hot chocolate, toasted marshmallows, and the Tale of the Glimmering Ghost?" he said, a twinkle in his eyes.

They all nodded. But the ranch foreman suddenly frowned and scratched his rough chin. "On second thought, maybe I'd better not tell it tonight."

"Why not?" asked Linda.

"Because"—Mac drew out the word as if reluctant to begin—"the story's not only true, but it happened on a night like this." He pointed to the sky. A full moon had just risen. It was peeking through the clouds, casting a mysterious glow over the treetops.

"And"—Mac paused, looking at the four faces staring at him—"it happened right here!"

"Here?" Kathy squeaked.

"Oh, come on, Kathy," Larry said in a cocky voice. "He's just trying to scare you. It didn't really happen on Coyote Mountain."

"Shhh." Linda hushed them. "Let Mac tell it!"

"All right," Mac said. "But don't blame me if you can't sleep tonight." He leaned toward the fire and motioned them closer.

"Twenty years ago, when I was just a young

ranch hand, there was a beautiful blond sixteen-year-old girl named Rachel Manlon. She lived with her brother, Glen, on the Flying Star Ranch."

"Glen Manlon?" Larry interrupted. "I know him. He comes into my folks' store." Larry's parents owned a leather and saddlery shop in Lockwood, the closest town to Rancho del Sol.

"Then this really is a true story," Linda said excitedly.

Mac nodded his head. Linda had never seen him look so serious, and a shiver of anticipation tingled up her spine. She pulled her goose-down vest around her and hunched closer to the fire.

"Rachel had a coal black mare named Glimmer," Mac continued. "She could run like the wind.

"Almost every afternoon, Rachel would take Glimmer out for a ride into the foothills. They loved to gallop off by themselves, and since Rachel was an excellent rider, her brother never worried about her getting hurt.

"Then one evening Rachel decided to take Glimmer out for a ride after dinner. It was still light out, so Glen didn't try to stop her. That was a big mistake."

"A mistake?" Linda asked. "Why?"

Mac lifted his eyes to look at her. "Because Rachel never returned to the ranch that night." He sighed deeply.

"As soon as Glen reported his sister missing, a search party was formed. For three days we combed the mountains and foothills. But there was no sign of Rachel or her horse. Not even a hoofprint!

"Well, folks in town got mighty suspicious. Had she really run off? they wondered. Or . . ."

He paused and poked the fire with a stick.

". . . or had something else happened to her?" He looked up, his eyes glowing in the firelight. Goose bumps raced up Linda's arms. She glanced over at Kathy. Her friend was staring at Mac, her eyes wide.

"Like what?" Larry asked.

"No one knows. Rachel and her horse just vanished into thin air, never to be seen again." Mac paused as if the story was finished. After a moment, he said, "Except . . ."

"Except what!" Linda demanded.

Mac lowered his voice to a gruff whisper. "I've never told this to anyone, but one night, about a week later, I was riding up this same mountain to look for a stray heifer.

"There was a full moon, just like tonight, so I could see pretty well. And it was real quiet. Not even the hoot of an owl or the chirp of a cricket.

"All of a sudden, I heard the pounding of hooves. I whipped around in the saddle, expecting to see another ranch hand, but there was nothing!

"Just as I was about to continue on, something made me look up at the top of the mountain. It was then that I saw it—a coal black horse, silhouetted against the moonlit sky. But when I blinked, it was gone!

"I figured I was just tired and seeing things. But later, other people in town started whispering about a riderless horse they'd seen racing across the countryside. And it came to be known as the Ghost Horse."

"Wow!" Linda exclaimed.

Suddenly, a loud rustle came from behind them. Startled, Kathy and Linda jumped to their feet and whirled around. A glowing face peered from behind a rock.

Kathy screamed in surprise, but Linda wasn't

fooled. It was only Larry, holding a flashlight under his chin.

"Very funny, Larry," she called out. He was always pulling stupid tricks.

With an eerie grin, Larry stepped from behind the rock. Still holding the flashlight, he crossed his eyes.

"I don't think anyone would ever mistake you for the beautiful Rachel Manlon." Bob chuckled, and even Linda had to laugh.

"Well." Mac stood up. "We'll be rising with the sun, so I suggest everyone get some sleep."

They all agreed, and Kathy and Linda headed for their sleeping bags.

"Did you believe Mac's story?" Kathy asked as they sat down and pulled off their boots.

"The first part, about Rachel disappearing—yes," Linda said. She took off her vest and rolled it up for a pillow. "But I don't know about Mac seeing a ghost horse. It seems a little too weird. Anyway, you know how Mac likes to exaggerate." She shrugged.

"Right. He probably just saw a deer," Kathy agreed. Quickly, she stuck her legs into her sleeping bag and pulled it up to her chin.

Linda snuggled into her own bag and tried to get comfortable.

"What do you think you'd do if you saw a ghost?" she asked Kathy. There was no reply. "Kathy?" Linda propped herself up on her elbows and looked over at her friend. Kathy's eyes were shut, and she was breathing softly.

With a sigh, Linda lay back down and stared up at the stars. It was no wonder Kathy had fallen asleep so quickly. They'd ridden four hours that day. Everyone was tired.

"Except me," Linda muttered to herself. Something about Mac's story kept rolling over in her mind. She'd heard plenty of his yarns before. But there was something really haunting about this one.

What *had* happened to Rachel and her horse? Where had they gone? They couldn't have just disappeared like that. Could they?

For a long while, Linda pondered the questions. Then her eyes grew heavy, and, with a yawn, she rolled onto her side and drifted off to sleep.

Linda was dreaming about the Ghost Horse when a strange noise, echoing through the treetops, woke her with a start.

She sat up and peered across the campsite.

The fire had died to flickering embers, but in the eerie light she could still tell that everyone was asleep.

She listened, waiting for the sound to come again, but the night was suddenly quiet. Too quiet. A spooky kind of quiet.

Linda shook her head. "You must have been dreaming," she told herself.

Ta-thump. Ta-thump. Thump, thump.

Linda's body tensed. There it was again, only this time she recognized the noise. It was the sound of a horse galloping.

Maybe one of the horses has broken free, she thought. I'd better check.

She unzipped her sleeping bag. Then she slipped on her vest and cowboy boots and silently tiptoed toward the grove of pine trees. When her eyes grew accustomed to the dark, she saw that all of the horses were still hitched to the rope she and Kathy had strung between two trees.

Then what's making that galloping sound? she wondered.

Amber began to paw the ground nervously. "Did you hear it too, girl?" Linda asked softly, smoothing her hand across the mare's silky neck.

Amber tossed her head, then pricked up her ears and stared at the top of the mountain. Linda followed her gaze, wondering what Amber was looking at.

Then she saw it, and her pulse began to race.

Ta-thump. Ta-thump.

A coal black horse, just like the one Mac had described, was galloping along the rocky ridge.

2 ♦♦♦♦

Linda raced through the grove of pines to get a better look. The moon shone brightly on the top of the mountain, and she could clearly see the jagged peaks. But the horse was nowhere in sight. It had vanished!

Now what should she do? She had to tell somebody!

She retraced her steps, stopping a moment to calm her nervous mare. "It's all right, girl." Linda gave Amber a soothing pat on the neck. "I promise nothing is going to happen to you." She reached into her vest pocket for one of the pieces of carrot she always carried with her.

"Here you go." She fed it to Amber. "See you in

the morning," Linda said, and headed back to her sleeping bag.

Kneeling next to Kathy, Linda shook her friend's shoulder.

"Kathy! Kathy!" she said in a low voice, not wanting to wake the others.

"Humph. Mumph," Kathy mumbled as she propped herself up on her elbows and blinked sleepily. She looked at Linda with a confused expression. "What're you doing up? What time is it, anyway?"

"I saw it!" Linda exclaimed.

"Saw what?" Kathy asked loudly, not sure she had heard right. "You mean the horse in Mac's story?"

"Shhh." Linda put a finger to her lips, then nodded. "It was galloping across the top of the mountain, just like Mac said!"

Kathy stared at her friend, then rolled her eyes and lay back down. "Oh, I get it. This is a joke. You're trying to scare me." She yawned and shut her eyes. "Well, it won't work."

Again, Linda shook Kathy's shoulder. "This isn't a joke!" she insisted. "I really saw it!"

"Sure, sure," Kathy muttered, unconvinced. "And I bet you saw a purple cow, too." She yawned again, flopped onto her stomach, and fell asleep.

Frustrated, Linda sat back on her heels. If Kathy didn't believe her, there was no use telling the others. They'd only laugh.

Reluctantly, she crawled across the foot of Kathy's sleeping bag and sat on her own.

Maybe what I saw wasn't the Ghost Horse, she thought as she took off her boots, but it was definitely a horse. Which was plenty strange, since Linda didn't think there were any wild mustangs in the area.

She snuggled down into her sleeping bag. She closed her eyes, hoping to fall asleep, but the image of the black horse kept racing through her mind.

Had someone been riding it? she wondered. No, she didn't think so. It would be foolish to go galloping over this rough country in the dark. It was too dangerous.

With a sigh, Linda rolled onto her side. It really was a mystery, and until she had proof that the horse even existed, she was going to keep the whole thing to herself.

Now, if only she could get some sleep.

"Hey, Linda! Wake up!" was the next thing she heard.

She opened her eyes. Larry, Bob, and Kathy were staring at her. Quickly, she sat up.

"Come on, sleepyhead," Larry said, poking her leg with the toe of his boot.

"You almost missed breakfast," Bob added with a grin. "I guess Mac's spooky tale must've really kept you tossing and turning."

Kathy laughed. "You're not kidding! Would you believe that in the middle of the night she woke me up to tell me she'd seen the Ghost Horse?"

Linda wriggled out of her sleeping bag. "Kathy!" she yelped in embarrassment.

"The Ghost Horse?" Larry and Bob chorused. They looked at each other and burst out laughing.

"Hey! You guys coming to breakfast?" Mac called from where he was squatting by the fire. "Oatmeal doesn't wait."

"We're coming!" Bob shouted. Then he turned

to Linda. "Must've been some wild dream," he said teasingly. Then he slapped Larry on the back, and the two boys headed over to Mac.

"It wasn't a dream," Linda mumbled as she knelt down and rolled up her sleeping bag.

"What did you say?" Kathy asked.

"Nothing." Linda shook her head. "I just wish you would believe me."

"Believe you?" Kathy gave Linda an incredulous look. "You mean you think you actually saw the Ghost Horse?"

"Maybe not the Ghost Horse," Linda admitted. "But I did see a horse galloping across the mountain."

Kathy's mouth dropped open. "Oh, come on, that's impossible. It must've been a shadow or . . ." Her voice trailed off. Then she said, "Well, maybe it was a coyote or some other animal."

Linda stood up. She knew her friend was trying hard to believe her wild story. She gave Kathy a smile.

"Come on. Let's get some breakfast." Linda turned, almost bumping into Larry.

"Have either of you seen my saddlebag?" he asked.

"Nope." The girls shook their heads and went to get a bowl of Mac's oatmeal.

"Buffalo Bill's secret recipe," Bob joked when Linda and Kathy sat down and looked at the gray, gooey lumps on their plates. He'd finished eating and was going to help Larry search for his saddlebag. "I'll check by the horses," Bob said.

Larry took off his cowboy hat and scratched his head. "I'm sure I put it down next to my sleeping bag last night, in case I got hungry."

"Hungry? What did you have in the saddlebag?" Linda asked.

"I brought along a couple of sandwiches," Larry admitted sheepishly. Everyone laughed.

"Maybe someone sneaked into camp and stole it," Kathy teased. Then she suddenly stopped eating and stared at Linda. "You don't think . . . ?"

Linda swallowed slowly, her mind racing. Could she have scared off a prowler last night?

"You don't think what?" Mac asked, not knowing what they were talking about.

"Linda claims she saw the Ghost Horse last night," Larry scoffed. "She figures it galloped into camp and ran off with my saddlebag clamped between its teeth." He laughed at his own joke.

"I didn't say it was the Ghost Horse," Linda protested. "I said I saw a *horse!*"

Mac hunkered down next to the fire and tipped back his hat. "You don't say," he murmured.

Then a shout made them all look up. Bob strode through the stand of pines, the saddlebag slung over his shoulder. "I found it!" he called. "A coyote dragged it about fifty feet up the mountain."

"A coyote!" Larry said. "Are you sure?"

"Yep. There were a couple of prints right beside it." Bob threw the bag to Larry, who caught it.

"Next time, remember to hang any bags containing food up in a tree," Mac told Larry.

Larry nodded, then turned to Linda. "Well, now we know the thief wasn't your mystery horse."

"Maybe not. But I still say I saw a horse on top of the mountain last night," she said before scooping up the last few bits of oatmeal.

By the time she had finished, the others were busy saddling their horses, and Mac was dousing the fire.

"You don't believe me either, do you, Mac?" Linda said when she saw a smile on his face. "If only there was a way I could *prove* it was a horse."

"There *is* one way to find out," he said.

"How—" Linda stopped her question as she guessed the answer. If Bob had been able to spot coyote tracks, there should be hoofprints, too.

She jumped to her feet and grabbed her gear. "Thanks for breakfast, Mac," she called over her shoulder as she hurried toward Amber.

The golden palomino was waiting eagerly and nickered a greeting when she saw Linda.

"Hi, girl!" Linda kissed Amber's velvety nose and slipped the reins over the mare's neck.

Amber stood still while Linda unbuckled the halter and quickly bridled her. Then, after brushing off the mare's coat, Linda lifted her western saddle onto Amber's back and tightened the girth.

Larry, Bob, and Kathy had already ridden down to a stream below the campsite. Mac was tying the cooking gear onto the packhorse.

"Don't wait for me," Linda called to him as she swung into the saddle. "I'll catch up with you."

He gave her a quick nod, then went back to his work. Grateful that he hadn't asked any questions, Linda waved to him, then squeezed Amber's sides with her heels.

Arching her neck, the palomino danced sideways, then settled into a jog as Linda guided her through the grove of pines. On the other side, they came into a clearing. Here Linda noticed a rough trail that snaked to the top of the mountain.

Probably made by animals going down to the stream, she thought. But it would also make a nice trail for a midnight rider!

Slowing Amber to a walk, Linda leaned to one side and searched the ground for prints. She found the coyote tracks and a scuff mark where the saddlebag must have been. But there were no hoofprints.

Giving Amber her head, Linda followed the twisting trail. Once again the scenery changed. Tall pines were replaced by scrubby spruce, and the ground became shaley and hard. On either side of the rough trail, treacherous drops and massive boulders made the going tough.

But Amber was as surefooted as a deer. She climbed toward the ridge that ran along the top of the mountain. When they reached a bank of rock just below the top, Linda halted the palomino. She dismounted and scrambled up the bank.

This was where she'd seen the Ghost Horse. But when she searched the ground, there wasn't even a broken twig or an overturned rock.

With a puzzled sigh, Linda let her eyes wander over the rugged terrain. At least the *view* is beautiful, so the ride hasn't been a total waste, she thought.

She continued to gaze down the steep mountainside into the valley beyond. It seemed to stretch for miles. No wonder Mac had wanted an early start. The stray cattle—or a mystery horse—could be anywhere.

Linda decided to give up the search. Maybe the others were right. It *had* been a coyote—and her imagination! She slid down the rock slope and remounted Amber.

Suddenly, the eerie neigh of a horse echoed across the rocky peaks.

Startled, Linda twisted in the saddle. But all she could see were the backs of the four riders as they headed north along the mountain ridge below her.

Had they heard the neigh, too? she wondered. Maybe she'd better catch up and find out.

But when Linda tried to urge Amber forward, the mare balked. Then she raised her head and nickered loudly into the wind.

Linda listened closely, but the only horse that answered was Patches, calling to the palomino.

"Come on, Linda!" Kathy hollered, waving her arm in the air.

"Let's go, girl." Linda kicked the mare gently, and this time Amber trotted forward, eager to join the other horses, who had halted on a nearby peak. Mac was peering through binoculars, scanning the foothills below.

"He's trying to spot the cattle," Kathy explained when Linda caught up to them.

"It would sure speed things up if I could spot some of those strays," Mac said. Abruptly, his head stopped moving, and he adjusted the lenses. "Well, well," he mused. "Looks like we've got a visitor."

"Someone else is riding up the mountain?" Linda asked, hoping that would explain the horse's neigh she'd heard.

"Not exactly." Mac handed her the binoculars. "More like driving. But it isn't a park vehicle."

"I see it. A jeep!" Bob pointed to the left. "Just below the rise," he said to Linda.

She looked through the binoculars and spotted the jeep just before it disappeared behind a rock wall. "Hey, it's gone!"

"Now, that's strange," Mac said.

"What is?" Larry asked.

"That jeep disappearing. This is park land, and vehicles are supposed to stay on the fire roads. But it looks to me like that jeep's *avoiding* the road."

"But why?" Bob asked.

Mac frowned. "It seems to me whoever's driving that jeep doesn't want anyone to know he's headed up the mountain!"

3♦♦♦♦

A few minutes later, the jeep bounced into view again. Linda squinted her eyes and adjusted the binoculars, trying to focus on the driver. But it was no use. Not only was the vehicle too far away, but it kept disappearing behind the trees and hills.

"Let me see!" Larry insisted. He reined Snowbird alongside Amber.

"Wait a minute!" Linda waved him away. The jeep had taken a sharp left, and she could see the door clearly. Something was written on it. "F-L," she read to herself. But before Linda could make out the rest of the letters, the jeep drove into a deep wash and vanished.

Slowly, Linda lowered the binoculars. "F-L," she repeated as she handed them to Larry.

"Thanks a lot! The jeep's gone!" he grumbled. But she ignored him. She was too busy trying to figure out what was printed on the side of the jeep. Florida? Flying?

Flying! That's what it was! The Flying Star Ranch! That was the name of Rachel and Glen Manlon's ranch!

Linda swung around in the saddle, eager to share her discovery with the others. Just as quickly, she stopped herself.

It was just a hunch that the letters *FL* were the first letters of Flying Star Ranch, and a wild hunch at that. Besides, why would Glen Manlon be driving up the mountain? Surely not to look for a Ghost Horse!

"Probably poachers hunting illegally on park lands," Mac remarked.

"Looks like it," Larry agreed as he handed the binoculars to Kathy.

"I'll bet they're after coyotes," Bob added. "Do you think we should report it?"

"When we get back, I'll check into it," Mac told him.

Kathy held up the binoculars. "Hey, look!" She pointed down the mountain. "Over there, in the valley next to the juniper thicket. I think I see some stray cattle!"

Mac took the binoculars from her. "That's them, all right. Good eyes, Kathy." He lowered the binoculars and put them in his saddlebag. "I'd guess they're about an hour's ride from here. Everybody ready?" he asked, looking directly at Linda.

She nodded eagerly. Chasing a few stray cattle would get her mind off the horse that didn't leave any tracks and the jeep with *FL* on its side. Maybe she'd forget about them altogether.

Single file, the riders carefully guided their horses down the steep slopes and sunbaked rocks. When they reached the foothills, the grass-covered ground sloped more gently, and they were able to pick up the pace.

They finally found the strays grazing in a sheltered hollow. The fifteen steers raised their heads and stared curiously, then continued cropping the stubby grass.

Mac laughed. "I don't think they're interested in running off, so let's take a break and stretch our legs."

They all dismounted, and Mac handed out soft

drinks. When they were finished, they climbed back onto their horses, and Mac gave them their orders.

"Linda, you and Larry ride on the right. Bob and Kathy, you two stay on the left. I'll drive them from behind. Don't let any of them break away, or the rest will try to follow."

He nodded, and the others guided their horses around the cattle, slowly boxing them into a tight bunch. Then, with whistles and shouts, they got the reluctant animals moving.

As they drove the cattle along the foothills to a pass in the mountain, Larry reined Snowbird next to Amber. The big Appaloosa pranced a few steps and swished his tail.

"What are you doing?" Linda asked.

Larry untied a rope from his saddle. "Getting ready in case one of the cows tries to run away." He made a loop at one end of the rope and held it up for her to see. "I'll lasso him."

"Hey, Larry! Show Linda your new trick!" Bob called from the other side of the herd.

Kathy looked at Larry and giggled. "When did you learn how to lasso?"

"I've been practicing," Larry said with a grin. "Now it's time to see if my practicing paid off."

Linda smothered a laugh.

"Just watch," Larry said, ignoring their teasing. He dropped the looped end of the rope by his horse's side and began to twirl it. The Appaloosa eyed the rope warily.

"All right," Linda agreed. "So you can twirl a lariat. Good trick, but that's not the same as roping a cow!"

"Pick one out!" Larry shot back. "Then watch a real cowhand at work."

Linda spotted a white-faced steer in the middle of the herd. She pointed. "That one," she said.

Larry turned Snowbird toward the milling herd of cattle. He waved the lariat above his head, then let it fly. It settled neatly around the white-faced cow's neck.

"How's that?" he asked proudly.

Bob and the girls clapped.

"Good toss," Mac said. Then he began to chuckle. "But how're you going to get your rope back?"

For a second, Larry frowned, then he tilted back his hat and shouted, "No problem!"

Clucking to Snowbird, he urged the Appaloosa between the cows until he reached the lassoed steer. Then he leaned over and tugged the rope from around its neck.

"How's that?" He held the rope up triumphantly.

As he did, the cattle began to surge nervously around Snowbird. Their heads bumped and banged against the horse's sides until, white-eyed with fright, Snowbird began to rear and pitch.

Startled, the cattle broke into a run.

"Whoa!" Larry shouted, frantically trying to calm his horse.

"Hang on!" Linda yelled as she sent Amber charging into the moving mass of animals.

As if the mare knew what was expected, she darted between the cattle, trying to drive them away from the frightened Snowbird. Linda held on tight and let Amber work. Finally, two steers broke away from the herd, creating an opening for Larry.

He spun his horse around, and with a powerful leap, Snowbird plunged to the left. He cantered after the two escaping cows, while Bob and Kathy flanked the herd, trying to slow the charging animals.

Larry reined in Snowbird and slid off his back. "Thanks, Linda," Larry said after a moment.

"Are you all right?" She looked down at him anxiously.

"I will be in a minute. As soon as I catch my breath." He wiped the dirt off his face. Then he ran a hand over Snowbird's flanks, checking to see that the Appaloosa was okay. "That sure was scary!"

"You can say that again." Linda laughed.

Larry looked up and smiled. "That sure was scary," he repeated. Then he shook his head and frowned a little. "I thought Snowbird was used to cows."

"He may be, but any horse would spook if a herd of cows crowded him like that," Linda explained.

"I guess you're right." Larry patted Snowbird's neck.

"Look, I'd better go help Kathy and Bob," Linda said. "Why don't you hang back until Snowbird calms down?"

She touched Amber with her heels, and the mare started after the herd, which had disappeared over a hill. For a moment, she and Amber loped along in silence, then Larry and Snowbird cantered up beside them.

"Afraid we would leave you behind?" Linda joked.

"No. Snowbird seems to want to run." Larry shrugged. "How about a race?"

Linda stared at him. "Haven't you had enough excitement? You almost stampeded the whole herd!"

"Afraid Snowbird will beat Amber?" Larry said, grinning.

"No! She'd win!" Linda answered confidently.

"Then why don't we make a little bet?"

Linda slowed Amber to a jog and looked over at Larry. "Like what?"

"If I lose, I'll clean your saddle and bridle."

Linda thought for a minute. She was definitely tempted. After the dusty ride, her tack would need a thorough soaping. And Snowbird did look as if he'd recovered from his scare.

"All right," she agreed, pulling up next to Snowbird. The Appaloosa arched his neck and stamped the ground impatiently. "Where to?"

Larry stood up in his stirrups. "Let's see. The herd looks like it's nearing the valley about a half-mile ahead. How about if we race to catch up to them? Whoever gets there first wins."

Half a mile wasn't a long distance, which probably gave Larry an advantage. Snowbird, with his choppy but powerful stride, always got off to a fast start. But Linda knew that he didn't have Amber's speed.

"Okay," she agreed, leaning forward in the saddle.

Sensing something was about to happen, Amber began to champ on the bit and dance in place.

"Ready! Go!" Larry yelled, and the Appaloosa leapt forward with a burst of speed.

Amber shot out after him, her hooves pounding the ground and her mane whipping the air like a banner. Soon she began closing in on Snowbird's heels.

Linda leaned farther forward in the saddle to give the mare a whisper of encouragement. It was all Amber needed. She stretched out her neck and lengthened her already long, smooth stride. By the time they came to a gentle incline, Amber had caught up to the powerful Appaloosa.

Neck and neck, they raced up the slope. But the moment they started down the other side, Amber's surefooted agility gave her the edge.

As the mare began to pull ahead, Linda could

hear Larry slap the Appaloosa with his reins. She could also hear the big horse's labored breathing. He was getting tired!

Gathering a fistful of Amber's mane, Linda loosened her hold on the reins. "Come on, girl, you can do it!" she shouted.

There was a sudden lurch from Amber, and Linda felt the mare's powerful muscles straining beneath her. If she could keep up this pace, Amber would surely win!

They were almost at the herd, when suddenly, out of nowhere, a small calf darted into Amber's path.

Unable to stop, the mare swerved sharply and lost her footing. She began to stumble—straight toward a deep gully!

4♦♦♦♦

With lightning-quick reflexes, Linda pulled back on the reins, bringing her horse's head up. The move helped Amber regain her balance in time to gather her powerful legs beneath her and jump.

Linda rose from the saddle, trying to go with the mare's motion. As they flew over the wide chasm, she caught a glimpse of the rocky bottom.

With a jolting thud, the mare's front legs landed on solid ground. But her hind hooves barely cleared the jagged edge of the gully.

Amber scrambled frantically for a foothold, but the shaley rock crumbled beneath her hooves. They were going to fall into the gully!

"Come on, girl!" Linda thrust her body forward.

The mare arched her neck and dug her front

hooves into the ground. At the same moment, her left hind foot found a small crevice, and with a lurch, she scrambled up and over the edge.

The sudden movement threw Linda onto the saddle horn, knocking the wind out of her. She doubled over, gasping for breath.

Amber slid to a halt. Her sides heaved, and her hind legs trembled from the effort of trying to regain her footing.

Moments later, Larry galloped up on Snowbird, a worried look on his face.

"Linda, are you okay?" He jumped to the ground before his horse had even stopped and ran up to her.

Still bent over, Linda nodded. "Yes," she gasped. "But check Amber."

With a careful eye, Larry checked the mare, running his hand over Amber's flanks and legs.

"Her back hooves are a little chipped," he said. "Nothing serious, though."

Linda straightened up, her breath coming easier.

"Whew! That was a close call," she said.

Larry nodded in agreement. "I didn't see everything—just Amber leaping across the gully. She's some horse," he said sincerely.

Linda laid her cheek against the mare's sweaty neck. "She would've won the race, too, if that calf hadn't darted in front of her," she told Larry.

He held up his hand. "Amber would've won fair and square. But only because Snowbird's out of shape," he added quickly.

"Then I won the bet?"

"Yep," Larry answered as he turned to Snowbird and mounted. "I'll clean your saddle and bridle."

"Great!" Linda smiled. "What time tomorrow?"

"Tomorrow?" Larry looked shocked. "You forget. I said I'd clean them; I didn't say *when*." And with a sly grin, he reined Snowbird around and cantered back the way he'd come, toward the place where the gully ended. "I'll round up that stray calf," he called over his shoulder.

Linda shook her head. That was just like Larry. She should have known better than to make a bet with him! But at least he was going back for the calf.

With a deep sigh, she hugged Amber around the neck. "I'm really proud of you," she told the mare. "But no more races today, I promise."

She urged Amber into a slow jog, trying to feel if there was any stiffness in the mare's gait. But the palomino moved out freely, and since she was eager to catch up to the others, Linda let her mare trot across the foothills toward the herd.

The next morning, Linda woke snug and comfortable in her own bed. With a sleepy yawn, she burrowed under the quilt, enjoying the soft mattress and pillow. It was hard to believe that last night she'd been sleeping on hard ground—with a rock digging into her side.

For a second she lay still. Then she kicked off the covers, jumped to the floor, and grabbed her jeans off the rocking chair. She dressed quickly.

She didn't want to miss breakfast. Not because she was that hungry but because she wanted to eat with her grandparents. They had been visiting friends in Lockwood the day before, so Linda hadn't had a chance to talk to them. And she wanted to find out more about Rachel Manlon and Glimmer. If anyone would know the real story of the Ghost Horse, it would be Bronco and Doña.

Since the death of their parents several years earlier, Linda and Bob had lived with Bronco and Doña Mallory. Linda and Bob loved their grandparents and had been very happy at Rancho del Sol.

Life at the ranch was never dull. And now there was the mystery of the Ghost Horse to solve!

Linda slipped moccasins onto her bare feet, then padded along the hallway toward the dining room.

The patio doors were wide open, and sun streamed into the dining room. Bronco and Doña were seated at the carved Spanish-style table, sipping coffee and reading the newspaper. Linda crossed the room and sat between them.

"Well, good morning!" her grandmother said with a warm smile, putting down her newspaper. "How're you feeling this morning?"

"Great, Doña!" Linda replied, helping herself to sliced oranges and mangoes. Her grandmother's real name was Rosalinda, but everyone called her Doña, which was a Spanish title of respect. "Boy, did that bed feel good," Linda added.

Tom "Bronco" Mallory, Linda's handsome, silver-haired grandfather, folded his newspaper and set it by his plate. "Getting soft, are you?" He chuckled. "We'll just have to toughen you up with a *real* cattle drive."

"Sounds good to me—as long as Mac doesn't cook!" Linda added with a laugh.

"Let me guess." Doña paused a minute, her

dark eyes twinkling. "He fixed pork and beans the way 'Uncle Harry' used to make them."

Linda stopped chewing. "How'd you know?"

"Oh, he's been telling that story for years," Bronco said, a grin on his rugged face.

"He told us another story—about a ghost horse," Linda said, looking up at them, her eyes wide with curiosity. "The story about Rachel Manlon."

For a second, her grandparents seemed puzzled. Then Doña nodded her head. "Oh, yes. That story. What a sad tale . . . and true!"

Linda sat on the edge of her seat. Now maybe she'd get some answers!

"I'm sure Mac added his extra touch of drama," Bronco said dryly as he finished his coffee.

"Can you tell me what really happened?" Linda asked.

"Well." Doña patted her dark, shining hair. Then she sat back and thought for a moment. "I remember it happened in the spring, because it was such a hard time for everyone. We'd had rain for two weeks straight, and all the ranchers—including the Manlons—lost livestock in the flooding."

Bronco leaned forward onto his elbows. "The Flying Star Ranch used to be one of the best spreads around," he said. "At one time, the Manlons bred the finest quarter horses in the state of California."

"Like Glimmer!" Linda exclaimed.

"Yes. That mare was something. She was beautiful, fast, and had lots of cow sense, too."

"That's right." Doña looked sad for a minute. "Rachel *and* the horse disappeared, didn't they? Ran away is what everyone thought."

"But why? And where'd they go?" Linda's head swung back and forth as she looked from one grandparent to the other.

Finally, Bronco shrugged his wide shoulders. "No one really knows. Her parents had been killed the winter before—a car accident. Then, when the floods ruined the barns and pastures . . . Maybe it just got to be too much for her. A number of folks gave up ranching that year and moved to the city."

Doña sighed and pushed her chair back. "That was a lot of tragedy for a sixteen-year-old girl to handle. And her brother, Glen, was under a great strain to keep the ranch going."

"What your grandmother means is Glen

couldn't be a parent to his sister *and* run the ranch. And since Rachel had a mind of her own, she started hanging around a rough crowd of kids."

"Which was a shame." Doña shook her head. "She was such a lovely girl. And what a horse-woman!"

"Almost as good as your grandmother *was.*" Bronco gave Linda a wink.

"Is!" Doña corrected her husband.

But Linda was only half listening to their exchange. She was too busy mulling over all the information they'd told her about the Manlons.

"So what about the Ghost Horse?" she asked.

"Oh, that's nothing more than a good campfire tale," Bronco said as he stood up.

"But Mac said he *saw* it!" Linda protested. And I think I did too! she wanted to add. But she didn't dare. Especially since she wasn't sure.

Bronco patted his granddaughter's shoulder. "You know how Mac loves to exaggerate," he said, and, with a wave goodbye, he strode out the door.

Linda set down her fork. "May I be excused?" she asked Doña. "I have to wash Amber down."

"Of course. And don't take the story so seriously. It happened such a long time ago. Everyone's forgotten about it by now."

"I guess," Linda said softly. She kissed her grandmother on the cheek, then ran outside to the barn.

As she gathered the necessary supplies to bathe Amber, she decided Doña was right. Probably everyone *had* forgotten about Rachel Manlon and Glimmer, and she needed to forget about them, too.

She attached a hose to the spigot and filled a bucket with warm water. She was trying out a special shampoo to help bring out the shine in Amber's coat. Not that Amber really needed it, Linda thought as she eyed the mare critically.

The palomino was grazing on the ranch's front lawn, and even with yesterday's dust in her coat, she was still beautiful. Her creamy white mane flowed thick and silky along her slender neck. Her well-muscled yet graceful body gleamed in the sunlight.

Linda whistled, and the mare picked up her head.

"Bath time!" Linda called.

Amber trotted over. Linda snapped a lead line to the halter and began to hose the mare off. Then she dipped a brush into the soapy water and scrubbed Amber's coat.

Enjoying the rubdown, Amber stuck her nose in the air and wiggled her lips. Linda laughed as she lathered the mare's stomach and flanks, then ran the sponge down her legs.

Fortunately, yesterday's accident hadn't caused any soreness. But Linda wanted to double-check. No, Amber's legs were free from swelling.

After rinsing off the mare's soapy coat, Linda began to lather her mane. Amber hated to get water in her eyes, so Linda was careful when she washed the palomino's forelock and star.

Last, she dropped the lead line and went around to the mare's hind end. Picking up the long tail, she dunked it into the bucket of soapy water.

Suddenly, Amber stepped forward, pulling her tail from the bucket. She swished it back and forth, and suds flew in the air.

"Hey! Where're you going?" Linda called. Then she saw Luisa, the Mallorys' cook and housekeeper, coming across the lawn.

Ears pricked with curiosity, Amber went to greet

the small, dark-haired woman. The mare knew Luisa would be carrying carrots in her pocket. Luisa was frightened of horses, but she had a soft spot for Linda's gentle palomino. Yet, even though Luisa liked Amber, she was careful to keep her distance from the mare.

The moment Luisa saw Amber coming toward her, she dug in her apron pocket for a carrot, then threw it into the grass as far away as she could.

Immediately, Amber went over to hunt for it. With one eye on the horse, Luisa waved at Linda.

"Phone call for you. It's Kathy!" Luisa called.

"Would you tell her I'm busy and I'll call her later?"

"She says it's very important," Luisa said, still keeping one eye on Amber. When she saw that the mare had eaten the carrot and was heading toward her, looking for more, she reached back into her apron pocket.

"Amber! Stop!" Linda commanded in a stern voice, though she had to muffle a laugh. Abruptly, the mare stopped and looked at her owner.

Luisa, seeing her chance, turned and hurried back to the house.

"You're really something, girl," Linda said when

she caught up to the mare. "Always getting into mischief. I'd better put you in the barn until I can rinse your tail."

Quickly, she stuck Amber in her stall, then ran into the house. She couldn't imagine what Kathy wanted that was so important.

Linda dashed across the kitchen to Bronco's office and picked up the phone there. "Kathy?"

"I thought you'd never get here! Guess what happened?"

But before Linda could answer, her friend started talking as fast as she could.

"There's a guy eating breakfast in my parents' restaurant, and when I was pouring his coffee, I overheard a conversation he was having with the man next to him. Guess what he said?"

"What?" Linda asked. She'd never heard her friend sound so excited.

"He said last night he'd seen a black horse galloping away from his ranch. And he called it the Ghost Horse!"

"He saw the Ghost Horse?" Linda repeated into the phone.

"Yes!" Kathy exclaimed. "At first I thought he was just joking, like Mac. But this guy wasn't smiling!"

For a second Linda was silent. Kathy's information had momentarily stunned her. Just an hour ago she'd been ready to forget all about the riderless horse on Coyote Mountain. Now someone else had seen it too!

"Linda? Are you still there?" Kathy asked on the other end of the phone.

"I'm here. But not for long! Amber and I will be at your place as soon as I rinse out her tail."

"Her tail?" Kathy echoed in a puzzled voice. But

Linda had no time to explain. She was too excited. Maybe if she could talk to this guy . . .

She said goodbye and hung up the phone. Then she scurried through the house, finally finding her cowboy boots by the tile-lined fireplace.

She kicked off her moccasins, slipped her bare feet into the boots, and raced from the house to the barn.

When she stepped into Amber's stall, holding the bridle and saddle, the mare gave her a questioning look.

"We're going into town," Linda told her. She checked to make sure Amber had completely dried off. Then she quickly bridled and saddled her horse.

She led Amber from the stall, stopping long enough to rinse the mare's soapy tail and turn off the hose. She'd just have to pick up the brushes and buckets later.

Riding the back trails, it didn't take Linda long to get to the Highway House, the Hamiltons' restaurant in Lockwood. Kathy was nowhere in sight, but when Linda rode Amber around to the barn, Patches hung his head over the corral fence and nickered a greeting.

"I'll put you in with your buddy only if you promise not to roll," Linda told the palomino as she dismounted.

Just then, Kathy dashed around the side of the house. Her freckled cheeks were flushed from running. "You made it!"

"I got here as fast as I could," Linda said as she undid the girth and slid the saddle off Amber's back. She swung the saddle onto the fence. "Is the guy still here?" she asked over her shoulder.

Kathy looked at her friend with a grimace. "He's gone."

"Gone!" Linda cried. "How could you let him get away?"

"What was I supposed to do? Tie him to the chair?" Kathy replied.

"No," Linda said, but she shook her head disappointedly as she led Amber into the corral.

Suddenly, Kathy grinned. "I did get his name, though."

Linda's face lit up. "You're wonderful! What is it?"

"It's Seth Wilson."

"I know him! He's a friend of Bob's!" With a whoop of excitement, Linda slammed the corral gate behind her. "His family owns a big ranch at the foot of Coyote Mountain."

"Where *you* saw the Ghost Horse!" Kathy announced.

"So now you believe me," Linda said, smiling.

Kathy looked hurt. "It's not that I didn't believe you. It was just that . . ."

"I know, it was such a wild story. Now tell me exactly what Seth said." Linda pulled Kathy down on a bale of hay under a large cottonwood tree.

Kathy settled herself comfortably, then began. "Well, he said that last night he was walking from his truck to the house when he heard a lot of noise by the barn. He was worried that one of the horses might be loose, so he went to check on them.

"When he opened the barn door, he heard the sound of galloping hooves. He ran around back just in time to see a black horse racing for the mountain!"

"Was anyone riding it?" Linda asked.

"He wasn't sure, but he thought he saw a girl clinging to its mane."

"Wow!" Linda gave a low whistle. "Did he have any idea who it was?"

Kathy shook her head. "I don't know, but he did call the black horse the Ghost Horse. And even though he said it jokingly, he *looked* pretty serious."

Linda propped her chin in her hand and thought for a moment. It had to have been the same horse she'd seen. But whose horse was it, and why was it galloping around at night?

"You don't think it has anything to do with Mac's story?" Kathy asked quietly.

"I don't know what to think," Linda replied. She was just as puzzled as her friend. "It can't be Rachel Manlon and Glimmer. They disappeared twenty years ago. Unless . . ."

"Unless what?"

Linda leaned closer and whispered, "What if Rachel's come back home?"

"Why would she do that?"

Linda shrugged. "I don't know. Maybe something happened twenty years ago that we don't know about. Something that would give her a reason to come back but not want to be seen."

Kathy shivered. "Stop it, Linda. You're scaring me!"

"That's it! Maybe she wants to *scare* somebody!" Linda jumped up from the bale of hay and started down the drive at a fast pace.

"Hey! Where are you going?" Kathy cried, running to catch up with her determined friend.

"To the office of the *Lockwood Gazette,"* Linda said, tossing the words over her shoulder as she headed for the sidewalk of Main Street. "To find out exactly what *did* happen twenty years ago!"

Minutes later, they were standing in front of a massive wooden desk, talking to the editor of the town's only newspaper.

"Back issues?" Mr. Freedman echoed Linda's question. "Sure. We've got them from the day the newspaper started—fifty years ago!"

"Can we see them?"

"Mind if I ask why?" He scratched his chin as he looked at the two girls.

Linda and Kathy looked at each other. "It's for a school project," Linda finally blurted out.

"Okay. Follow me." Mr. Freedman led the girls out of his office.

Kathy and Linda followed him into a huge storeroom. When he flicked on the lights, both girls gasped. Every inch of the room was covered with shelves stacked with newspaper-sized leather binders.

"This could take a week!" Kathy groaned.

"It's not as bad as it looks," Mr. Freedman assured her. "They're arranged according to year."

"We're looking for issues from twenty years ago," Linda said.

He put on a pair of glasses and began walking through the maze. "Ah, here we are." He stopped at a row of shelves. "January's issues start at the bottom. December's end up here."

"Thank you!" Linda strode eagerly to the shelves.

Mr. Freedman slid his glasses back to the top of his head. "My pleasure. And good luck," he added as he left them alone.

"We'll need it," Kathy muttered as she stared dejectedly at the stacks of binders.

Undaunted, Linda was already checking the dates on the spines. "Doña said Rachel disappeared in the spring. That'll narrow it down."

"Oh, good. Now it will only take two days instead of a week," Kathy said sarcastically.

"Here's March. Give me a hand with these."

Linda and Kathy removed the March volumes from the shelf and placed them on the floor.

"You do March, and I'll look through April," Linda said, pulling out another volume.

Wrinkling her nose, Kathy held the large binder away from her. "Phew! I think mice have been living in these."

"You're supposed to read them, not smell them," Linda teased her friend.

Kathy plopped down on the floor. Linda knelt down beside her. "What're we looking for, anyway?" Kathy asked.

"An article about Rachel's disappearance," Linda told her without glancing up. "It had to have made the front page. I mean, twenty years ago it was probably the most exciting thing that happened in Lockwood. Get these headlines." She pointed to a page. "'Rancher's Cows Crash Square Dance.'"

Both girls began to giggle. Suddenly, Linda cried out, "Here's something!"

Kathy moved closer to Linda. "Where?"

Linda pointed to big, bold letters. "'Local Girl

Disappears,' " she read out loud. " 'Brother Held for Questioning.' "

"Wow!" Kathy gasped. "Read more!"

" 'Early yesterday morning, local rancher Glen Manlon reported his sister, Rachel Manlon, missing. He told the sheriff she'd ridden out the previous night on her horse and hadn't returned.'

"Then the article goes on to say—'Following up on a report by two eyewitnesses, who claim to have seen the brother and sister arguing the previous afternoon, Sheriff Lawson went to the Manlon ranch to investigate. He reportedly found blood on the kitchen floor.' "

"Blood!" Kathy's eyes flew open.

" 'Mr. Manlon was taken in for questioning and is still being held.' That's the end of the article." Linda quickly began turning pages.

"Wait! I have it!" Kathy yelled. " 'Brother Released for Lack of Evidence,' " she read.

"Whose blood was it?" Linda asked.

"Uh . . . here it is. 'Lab tests prove the blood was Mr. Manlon's. He said it was from a nosebleed he'd gotten in a brawl the night his sister disappeared.' " Kathy looked expectantly at Linda.

"He argued with his sister, then later that night got into a fight." Linda bit her lip as she puzzled over the information. Then, abruptly, she began turning pages again.

"We need to find out what Rachel and Glen Manlon argued about," she told Kathy. "It might be the key to the mystery of the Ghost Horse!

"Here's more. On page two." Linda began reading. " 'Attempts to locate Rachel Manlon have proved futile. Search parties have been discontinued. A missing-persons bulletin has been posted to all major cities.'

"Which obviously didn't turn up anything," Linda said.

"Just like us. We haven't really found out anything, either." Kathy stood up with a groan and began reshelving the newspapers. "Boy, am I ever tired and hungry and—"

"I get the picture." Linda interrupted with a laugh as she began helping her friend put back the binders.

On their way out of the newspaper office, they waved to Mr. Freedman, who was busy talking on the phone. When they opened the outside door, they were greeted by the bright midday sun.

"How about a soda? My treat," Linda said.

"Sounds good . . . Hey!" Kathy grabbed Linda's shoulder. "There's Seth Wilson! Coming out of the bank."

Linda stood on tiptoe, trying to see over the cars. Then she hooked her arm through Kathy's and began dragging her across the street. "Quick! Before he gets away again!"

Seth Wilson was standing at the door of the bank, counting money in an envelope. Linda took the steps two at a time, stopping at the top so quickly that Kathy crashed into her side.

"Seth? Hi, I'm Linda Craig. Bob's sister."

He glanced down at her. "Oh, yeah. Hi," he said in an uninterested voice. He turned back to the envelope and continued to leaf through his money.

Linda pulled Kathy forward. "This morning you were at the Hamiltons' restaurant talking about a mysterious horse?"

Seth stopped counting, and this time when he looked at Linda, his expression was one of interest. "Yeah. Strangest thing I ever saw."

"Who do you think it was?" Linda asked.

Seth tipped back his cowboy hat and thought a

minute. "Did you ever hear the story of the Ghost Horse?" he finally asked.

Both girls nodded.

He bent closer. "Well, my dad was telling me about it this morning, and if you ask me, the girl on that horse was Rachel Manlon!"

Suddenly, a dark-haired man pushed Linda aside and grabbed Seth by the collar.

"Well, nobody asked you your opinion, Seth Wilson!" he growled. "So just keep it to yourself!"

6

"Hey! Look out!" Linda protested as she stumbled down the steps of the bank.

Kathy reached out and steadied her friend with a hand under her arm. "That's Glen Manlon!" she whispered, pointing toward the broad-shouldered man who still had Seth by the collar.

Linda looked up in time to see Manlon shove Seth backward. Then Manlon pushed open the doors and strode into the bank.

"You're kidding!" Linda exclaimed, leaping back up the steps. Seth was still standing by the double doors, staring at them in stunned silence.

"That was Rachel's brother!" Linda told him excitedly.

"Yeah, I know," Seth said. "And, boy, was he mad!"

"I wonder why," Kathy said.

Seth straightened the front of his shirt. "Maybe he's still touchy about his sister running away. Though after twenty years, you'd think he would've gotten over it."

He started down the steps. Linda and Kathy followed him.

"Probably all the talk about the Ghost Horse stirred up some bad memories," Linda said.

"Could be," Seth agreed. "But whatever it is, I'm not sticking around to find out." With a nod goodbye, he took off down the sidewalk.

Kathy tugged on Linda's sleeve. "Come on. We'd better get out of here, too."

"Okay." Linda took one last look at the bank. "I wonder where Glen Manlon came from. I never even heard him come up the steps."

"I saw his jeep when we crossed the street," Kathy said.

"His jeep! Why didn't you tell me?"

"I couldn't. You were dragging me up the steps too fast!"

"Where is it?" Linda looked right and left.

"Over there." Kathy led her to a tan jeep parked by the curb. On the side of the door, the words "Flying Star Ranch" were printed in bold white letters.

Linda grabbed Kathy's arm. "That's the jeep we saw on Coyote Mountain!" she cried.

Kathy's face turned pale beneath her freckles. "What was *he* doing up there?"

Linda was about to guess at an answer when she glimpsed Manlon coming out of the bank.

Quickly, she clapped a hand over Kathy's mouth and yanked her into the doorway of the drugstore.

"Hey! What are you doing?" Kathy mumbled.

"Shhh. It's him." Linda nodded toward the jeep. Glen Manlon was walking toward it with determined strides.

Leaning slightly forward, Linda peered around the edge of the doorway, trying to see him better. But all she caught sight of was a grim mouth beneath the shadow of his cowboy hat.

Manlon climbed into the jeep, slammed the door, and started the engine. But he didn't drive off.

Linda ducked back into the doorway. "I think he saw me!"

Both girls flattened themselves against the building and held their breath. Finally, they heard a motor roar and then fade as the jeep pulled away from the curb and zoomed up the street.

"Whew!" Kathy gasped. "That was close!"

"I'll tell you one thing," Linda said as they started back toward the Hamiltons'. "Glen Manlon's acting very suspicious!"

"Do you think he's hiding something?" Kathy asked. "Maybe *he* knows something about the Ghost Horse!"

"Or he's trying to find out—just like we are," Linda said. "Which is why he was driving around Coyote Mountain yesterday. I'll bet he thinks the answer lies up there." She stopped in front of a soda machine and dropped in some coins.

"Well, I'm ready to ride up there and look," Kathy said enthusiastically.

"Great!" Linda handed her friend a cold can of soda. "Now let's go back to your barn and make plans."

* * *

The next day, the two girls wound their way back up the old miner's trail. When they neared the ridge that ran along the top of the mountain, they began searching among the scrubby spruce.

They weren't sure what they were looking for, but they were hoping to find some clue that would lead them to the Ghost Horse.

There was nothing.

"I'll bet Manlon didn't find anything either," Linda said in a discouraged voice.

"Maybe we'll feel better after we eat lunch," Kathy suggested.

Linda nodded in agreement. The girls guided their horses back down the narrow path to the campsite where they'd camped overnight on the roundup.

"I'm starving." Linda slid off Amber and pulled a sack of food from her saddlebag.

Kathy dismounted, too, and both girls loosened the girths on their saddles. Then they took off the bridles so the horses could graze.

Straddling the log beside the ashes of Mac's campfire, they ate in silence. Linda was puzzling over the fact that there weren't any clues, when she suddenly stopped chewing her sandwich. Wrinkling her brow, she peered closely at the cleared area around the campsite. Then she nudged Kathy with her elbow.

"The day we rode out, didn't we leave a big pile of dead wood over there?" she asked her friend.

Kathy took a sip of her drink and thought for a moment. Then she nodded. "You're right."

"Which means . . ." Wide-eyed, the girls stared at each other.

". . . somebody's been here," Kathy finished in a scared whisper.

Just then, a loud rustle made them jump in surprise. Linda twisted around on the log and looked behind her.

Amber was peering at a thicket of thorny bushes. Snorting and blowing, the mare didn't know whether to be curious or afraid.

Slowly, the girls set their sandwiches on the log and stood up. Linda put a finger to her lips and began to move cautiously toward the bushes. Kathy tiptoed behind her friend, holding tightly to Linda's sleeve.

Amber took a hesitant step forward and pawed

the ground. With a scared yip, a little brown-and-white-spotted dog scooted out from behind the bushes. He was limping.

Linda grabbed Amber by the mane and told her to calm down. The palomino planted her feet, then stretched out her neck and sniffed curiously at the dog.

"Gee, I wonder where he came from?" Kathy said. "There isn't a house for miles."

"He looks hungry." Linda picked up her peanut butter sandwich and tore off a piece. When she held it out, the dog darted over, grabbed a bite, and gobbled it down.

"It's a good thing we brought plenty of food!" Kathy said as the dog ate the rest of Linda's sandwich, then hungrily gulped down Kathy's hard-boiled egg.

When he'd finally eaten enough, the dog sat back on his haunches and wagged his tail.

"I think we've made a friend," Kathy said. She knelt down and patted her leg. "Here, boy," she said. This time the little dog came right up to her and licked her on the cheek.

Linda bent down and scratched behind his floppy hound's ears. "There's no collar. I wonder who he belongs to."

Gently, she picked up his paw. "Look, he's got a small cut. I think we should take him home and let Mac doctor it."

"Good idea. Maybe we can find out who owns him, too," Kathy said. Then she began giggling as the dog flopped onto his back and began vigorously rolling in the dirt.

"Come on, dusty dog," Linda called. "You can ride with me."

"Dusty. That's what we ought to call him," Kathy said.

"That's a perfect name!" Linda said with a laugh as the dog stood up and shook, spraying dust everywhere.

They caught the horses, bridled them, and tightened the girths.

After Linda mounted, Kathy handed the little dog up to her. Cradling him with one arm, Linda held him in her lap.

For a minute, he squirmed against her. Then he rested his chin in the crook of her elbow and closed his eyes.

"It seems like he's used to riding on a horse," Kathy commented.

When they finally reached the ranch, Linda's arm was stiff, but Dusty was sleeping comfortably.

Kathy looked at her watch. "Uh-oh, I've got to get going. I promised Mom I'd help her make chili. It's the special at the restaurant tonight."

"I'll see you tomorrow." Linda waved goodbye to Kathy, who was urging Patches down Rancho del Sol's long drive. Linda guided Amber toward the barn.

"What've you got there?" Mac met them in the aisle. He held up his hands, and Linda gladly gave him the little dog. Dusty wiggled in the foreman's strong arms, then licked his face.

"Friendly, isn't he?" Mac laughed as he dodged the pink tongue.

"His front paw's cut," Linda told Mac as she dismounted.

Mac rotated the paw, studying it. "No problem. A little ointment will fix it good as new."

He carried Dusty to the barn's medicine cabinet, while Linda unsaddled Amber and led her into her stall.

She was brushing the palomino's back, when Mac leaned over the door. Dusty was still in his arms.

"Where'd you get him?" Mac asked.

"Kathy and I found him on Coyote Mountain. By the campsite."

"And what were you girls doing up there?" he asked, a grin on his weathered face. "Looking for ghosts?"

Linda nodded as she gave Amber one last stroke with the brush. Mac might be making a joke, but she was beginning to think he was right.

When she opened the stall door, Mac set Dusty on the ground. The little dog ran over and jumped up on Linda, putting his front paws on her leg.

"He's better already," she said. "And after something to eat, he'll really feel good."

She thanked Mac, whistled to Dusty, and headed for the ranch house. It was almost dinnertime, and she was hungry too!

But when Luisa saw the little dog, she shooed him from the kitchen.

"No animals in my kitchen!" she scolded. "And he sleeps in the barn, not in your bed, Linda!"

"Don't worry," Linda promised. "He won't

sleep in my bed." She grinned at Luisa. "And, since I'm dining alone, I'll eat with Dusty out on the patio." Doña and Bronco were dining with friends, and Bob was at Larry's.

Linda picked up Dusty and carried him around to the patio. When they got there, Luisa had just placed Linda's dinner on the table. Beside Linda's plate was a paper plate for Dusty.

"Thanks, Luisa," Linda said with a grin.

The housekeeper rolled her eyes and went back inside the house.

Linda dished out a portion of enchiladas and beans onto the paper plate.

"You must be a Mexican dog," she said as Dusty wolfed down the food. "But I know you'd rather eat peanut butter sandwiches!"

After Dusty had polished off the last bite, Linda thought about what to do with him. She'd give him a quick bath and then sneak him into her room. Of course, he wouldn't sleep in her bed. She'd promised Luisa!

Later, when she was tucked under her quilt, Linda propped herself on one elbow and looked at the little dog. He was curled up on the Mexican rug, his tail wrapped around his nose.

Not only had he charmed Bronco and Doña that evening, but he'd enjoyed his bath. And he hadn't objected to the rolled-up kerchief Linda had tied around his neck for a collar. In fact, he enjoyed being fussed over so much that Linda could tell he was used to that kind of attention—which meant he had to be somebody's pet. But whose? And what had he been doing on the mountain?

Something told her Dusty was connected with the missing firewood and the black horse. Maybe he was even the clue they'd been searching for.

As if he knew she was thinking about him, Dusty wagged the end of his tail, then shut his eyes and began to snore.

Linda lay back and shut her eyes, too. Maybe she'd come up with some answers in the morning.

Crash!

Linda woke with a start and sat up in bed. What was that? She stared across the pitch black room. Someone was banging at her door!

But it was only Dusty, leaping at the knob with his front paws.

"Dusty! Here, boy!" Linda called softly, afraid the racket would wake up her grandparents.

"Dusty!" She knelt at the foot of the bed and called again. The little dog stared imploringly at her, then began frantically scratching at the door.

Linda slid out of bed. "What's wrong?" she asked in a whisper, reaching to calm him with a pat.

A loud crash and the sound of running footsteps made her hand freeze in midair.

That's what Dusty had been trying to tell her.

Someone was in the house!

7 ♦♦♦♦

As soon as Linda opened her bedroom door, Dusty dashed between her legs and scampered down the hallway.

"Dusty!" she called urgently. "Come back!"

She started after the dog just as Bob flung open his door and stepped into the hall. Linda ran smack into his shoulder.

"Be quiet!" he whispered hoarsely, catching her so she wouldn't fall. "There's someone in the kitchen!"

"I know! And Dusty went after him! Come on!"

They padded down the stairs in their bare feet and pajamas and rushed through the dining room, skidding to a halt in front of the kitchen doorway.

Linda's pulse was racing. What if the intruder was still in there!

She glanced at Bob. He put a finger to his lips and slowly edged forward. Like a shadow, Linda moved with him. Cautiously, they poked their heads through the open doorway and glanced right, then left.

Except for Dusty, the kitchen was empty.

Linda let out her breath in a whoosh of air. Even Bob straightened up with a relieved sigh.

"Whoever it was must've run out in a hurry," he said, pointing to the unlatched top of the Dutch door. "I'm going to see if they're still around."

He went into the mudroom to put on his boots. Linda walked over to Dusty.

The little dog was standing by the refrigerator, sniffing at something on the floor. Linda knelt next to him. On the floor was a jar of peanut butter.

"The prowler wanted peanut butter?" Linda said in disbelief.

"Prowler! What prowler?" A voice boomed behind her, and the overhead light switched on. Blinking sleepily, Bronco and Doña came into the kitchen, hugging their bathrobes around them.

Linda jumped up. "Someone broke into the house!"

"And I'm going after him," Bob added. He strode from the mudroom, boots on his bare feet and a jacket over his pajamas.

"Not by yourself!" Bronco told him.

All of a sudden, a loud neigh came from outside.

"That's Amber!" Linda cried, and without a moment's hesitation, she threw open the bottom half of the Dutch door and raced out. What if the prowler was after her horse?

With Dusty barking at her heels, Linda ran for the barn.

"Wait for us!" her grandfather called, but nothing was going to slow her down. Not even the sharp stones from the drive digging into her feet.

Another neigh rang out, and Dusty took off around the barn. It was then Linda remembered—Amber wasn't in her stall. Mac had turned her out in the small corral!

Linda crossed the drive and followed Dusty around the barn. She reached the barn just in time to see a black horse gallop past the machine shed and disappear down the path into a stand of pine trees.

Dusty raced after it!

"Dusty!" Linda called. "Dusty!"

The little dog stopped and looked back at Linda, then stared longingly down the path. Linda ran up to him and grabbed hold of the kerchief around his neck.

Just then, Bob ran up to her. "What's going on?"

"It was the Ghost Horse!"

Bob stared at his sister in disbelief, but Linda had no time to explain.

"Here! Take Dusty. And *don't* let him go after the Ghost Horse! I have to check on Amber."

She ran back to the corral and saw Amber standing by the fence, watching all the commotion. Linda climbed the lowest board and patted the mare's golden neck.

"Thank goodness you're all right," murmured Linda. Whoever it was, the intruder had obviously not been after her horse. Amber must have been just whinnying an alarm, telling the household there was a stranger on the property. Except . . .

Linda thought for a moment, trying to picture the horse galloping off. Had someone been riding it?

"Now, tell me again what you saw," Bob said as he walked up to her. He was carrying the squirming dog under one arm.

At the same time, Bronco and Doña came around the barn.

"Would you two quit dashing off and tell us what's going on!" Bronco growled.

"Linda, you could have been hurt!" Doña scolded. "Running after a prowler by yourself, and barefoot, too!"

Linda jumped off the fence. "It was a black horse!" she explained breathlessly. "Like the one I saw on the mountain and the one Seth Wilson saw at his ranch."

"Hold on." Bronco raised his hand. "Backtrack and tell us the whole story."

Linda took a deep breath. Then, as they walked slowly back to the house, she told her grandparents everything, even her suspicions about Glen Manlon.

"You mean that was *his* jeep we saw on the mountain?" Bob asked.

"Yes. And you should've seen how mad he was at Seth. He grabbed him right by the collar like this." She demonstrated on her brother's jacket.

"I don't know." Doña shook her head. "It's hard to believe that the horse you saw is connected with the Manlons."

"I agree with Doña." Bronco ushered them into the kitchen. "It's probably some kid playing tricks. Who else would be stealing peanut butter?"

"Are you going to call the police?" Bob asked.

"Since nothing was taken, we'll report it in the morning," Doña answered with a yawn. "Now, let's all get back to bed."

Bronco and Doña said good night and headed for their room. Linda hung back with Bob. Her brother set Dusty on the kitchen floor. When he was free, the little dog trotted over to the door and whined.

For a second, Linda watched him. Then she turned to Bob. "Dusty wanted to go after the horse," she told her brother. "Do you think he knows the prowler?"

Bob shrugged. "Who knows? Maybe he could lead us right to him—or her."

"Then you'll help me?" Linda asked eagerly.

"It depends. What do you plan on doing?"

Linda bent down and scratched the little dog behind the ears. "We could take him partway up

Coyote Mountain and let him go. Then follow him."

Bob thought for a second. Dusty looked up at him and wagged his tail so hard it thumped like a drum on the floor.

Bob laughed. "Okay. But let's leave early. If it *is* a wild-goose chase, I don't want to waste the whole day."

After an early breakfast the next morning, Bob and Linda headed across the mesa toward Coyote Mountain. By now, Amber knew the way when they reached the foothills, and she eagerly led Rocket up the old miner's trail.

Again, Dusty rode with Linda. But this time the little dog didn't fall asleep. He sat perched on her lap, his front paws balanced on the seat of the saddle.

When they neared the old campsite, he began barking and whining. Linda halted Amber and, with both arms, began to lower the little dog. Wiggling from her grasp, he jumped to the ground, then took off like a flash.

Linda and Bob followed him as closely as they could. Dusty swam across a stream, then clambered up its steep bank. He disappeared in the thick undergrowth on the other side.

"Where'd he go?" Bob called to Linda.

"I don't know!" She urged Amber into the swiftly running water.

The mare sloshed upstream until they came to a break in the undergrowth. Then Linda urged Amber up the steep bank. She could hear Rocket splashing behind her.

Beside them, the mountain rose sharply to sheer rock and jutting ledges.

"Did we lose him?" Bob reined in Rocket beside the palomino.

"I think so," Linda said, nodding.

Just then, they heard a bark.

"Wait! That's him!" Linda urged Amber into a slow trot. Ahead of them, Dusty darted from behind a pile of boulders, barked again, then vanished.

This time Amber didn't need any urging. Tilting her ears forward, she trotted rapidly across the rough ground until they reached the boulders. Then she stopped. In front of them was the entrance to a cave.

Bob pulled up beside Linda and quickly dismounted. "Lucky I brought a flashlight," he said, dropping the reins and digging in his saddlebag.

With a whoop of excitement, Linda slid off Amber. She couldn't believe they'd finally found something!

Bob flicked on the light. The cave opening was small and narrow, and the two of them had to crawl inside on their hands and knees. About ten yards into the dark tunnel, they were able to stand up.

"At least it's nice and dry in here," Bob whispered.

"A good place for a midnight prowler to hide out!"

Slowly, they worked their way deeper into the cave.

"I think I see something ahead," Bob finally said. "Come on!" Flashing the light before him, he ducked into a small cavern. In the middle of the dirt floor was a knapsack and the cold remains of a fire. Behind it, Dusty was nestled on a rolled-up sleeping bag.

He greeted them with a friendly bark.

"Wow!" Linda exclaimed as she looked around. "Someone's been living here!"

Bob bent down and flipped open the knapsack.

"For a couple of days, it looks like. There are a bunch of empty food cans in here." He held one up. "Including dog food cans!"

"And look what I found!" Linda said excitedly. She picked up a halter and proudly displayed it. "*Now* do you believe I saw a horse and not a coyote that night?"

Bob chuckled. "Yeah, I believe you. But you'll need more proof than that to convince Larry."

"I'd like to find the *real* horse, too!" Linda added.

Suddenly, Dusty jumped off the sleeping bag and scurried out of the cavern.

"Somebody must be out there!" Linda dropped the halter and took off after him, almost bumping her head on a low-hanging rock.

"Here! Take the flashlight," Bob said, tossing it to her.

She pointed the light down the tunnel and ran as far as she could. Then, dropping down on all fours, she crawled out of the cave. Bob was right behind her.

When they stood up, they found themselves face to face with a young blond girl astride a coal black horse.

For a moment, the girl stared at them, wide-eyed with surprise. Then she wheeled the horse around and bolted for the top of the mountain.

Quick as a flash, Linda grabbed Amber's reins and vaulted into the saddle. The mare immediately sprang forward, with Bob and Rocket and Dusty right on her heels. Linda knew she couldn't lose the girl and the horse now! Not when they were so close!

But as Amber galloped after it, the black horse swerved sharply to the left and vanished behind an outcropping of rock.

Linda, thinking she could cut them off, guided Amber through a maze of boulders. Twisting and turning, the mare dodged between the massive rocks as if she were cutting cattle from a herd. But when Amber rode out of the rocks, Linda saw that the black horse was still in front.

Suddenly, the steep ridge that ran along the top of the mountain loomed before her. Amber tried to plunge up a bank, but she slipped backward. With a gentle tug on the reins, Linda pulled her horse around. Even though it meant losing the other girl, she couldn't risk injuring Amber.

Linda looked up, expecting to see the black

horse slowing, too. But, like a jackrabbit, it bounded up the bank of rock. Then, as if it had wings, the horse flew over the top of the mountain and disappeared from sight.

Linda couldn't believe her eyes. How had the black horse made it up there?

She twisted in the saddle, about to wave to Bob to stay back, when a frightened scream made her freeze.

The cry for help was coming from the other side of the mountain!

Linda jumped off Amber as Dusty came running up, barking loudly.

"Bob!" she yelled to her brother. "That girl must be in trouble!"

Leaving Amber ground-tied, Linda began to make her way up the bank of rock. Grabbing hold of the trunk of a stunted spruce, she pulled herself up to the crest of the ridge. Then she climbed along a flat rock and peered over the edge.

About fifteen feet below her, Linda saw the black horse. The horse had lost its footing and was sliding down the mountain. The blond girl was clinging to its mane, her face white with fear.

The black horse frantically scrambled sideways, trying to regain its footing. But the shaley rock crumbled beneath its hooves, and the horse fell to its knees.

"Help!" the girl cried.

Suddenly, the horse's hind legs slid out from under it. With a heavy thud, the animal fell, pitching the girl over its neck.

Without its rider's weight, the black horse was able to lurch to its feet. It lunged toward the top of the mountain. And as it did, the force of its hooves sent a miniature avalanche of brittle rocks raining onto the girl.

The ground began to slide out from under her. The terrified girl reached out and clutched a tree root.

"Help!" she cried again.

"Bob!" Linda screamed. "Get your rope!" Then she leaned over the ledge and called to the girl to hang on.

Bob ran up to the ledge, his lariat over his shoulder. Dusty was right behind him. Quickly, Bob tied a loop in one end of the rope and threw it down to the girl.

With a cry of relief, she grabbed hold of the loop.

"Hang on!" Bob hollered. "We'll pull you up!"

Linda caught the slack rope in her arms and half ran, half slid back down the bank of rock to Amber. She wrapped the rope end several times around her saddle horn, then secured it with a knot.

Clucking to Amber, Linda led the mare forward until the rope was taut.

"Tell me when!" she called up to Bob.

He waved her on. "Go ahead and pull!"

"This is it, girl. Easy now." Linda gently tugged on the reins.

As they walked slowly forward, Linda kept one hand on Amber's bridle and the other on the rope. She could feel it vibrate beneath her fingers. She hoped it wouldn't break.

"About five more feet!" Bob called. "Then I'll be able to reach her!"

Linda patted Amber's neck. She knew how hard it would have been to pull the girl up without the mare's help.

"Okay, stop!" Bob suddenly hollered. Linda halted the palomino and moved backward to watch her brother. He was lying on his stomach, his head and chest draped over the ridge.

Linda saw Bob extend his body, reaching for the girl. Then she caught a glimpse of blond hair and a red shirt as Bob pulled the girl halfway onto the ridge.

For a second the girl lay still, and Linda wondered if she was all right. Then Linda saw her lift herself the rest of the way up.

Wagging his tail, Dusty greeted the girl with a big kiss.

The rope went slack, and Bob signaled Linda to untie it. Quickly, she darted back to Amber and undid the knot. Then she coiled the rope and retraced her steps up the bank of rock.

When Linda reached the crest, the girl was sitting on the rocky ground, still trembling.

Curious, Linda stared at her. She was small and very thin. Linda thought she looked to be about fourteen years old, but it was hard to tell, since her hair and face were streaked with dirt.

"Are you okay?" Linda asked.

The girl nodded, then looked up with a worried expression.

"How's Cinder?" she asked.

"Your horse?"

"Yes. I hope she didn't hurt herself when she fell."

Bob took the rope from Linda. "I'll go check," he offered, winding up the rest of the rope. "She's down by Rocket, my horse."

"Thanks," the girl said. Then she smiled gratefully at Linda. "You, too. I don't know what I would have done if you hadn't been here to help me."

"You didn't look too happy when you saw us coming out of the cave."

"That's because you scared me half to death!"

"Well, you gave us a pretty good scare, too!" Linda exclaimed, and they both started laughing.

Then Linda extended her hand. "I'm Linda Craig."

"I'm Kelly Michaels." The girl shook Linda's hand, then tried to stand up. But the moment she put weight on her right leg, she fell back with a cry of pain.

Tears immediately filled her eyes. "I think I must have twisted my ankle." She rolled up her pants leg and pulled off her sneaker and sock. Her ankle was already very swollen.

"Sit tight a minute," Linda told her. "I've got some stretch bandages in my saddlebag."

Bob had just finished checking out Kelly's horse when Linda ran up to Amber and started digging in her saddlebag.

"What are you looking for?" he asked.

"First-aid kit. Kelly twisted her ankle—here it is!"

Kelly was sitting quietly, Dusty curled in her lap, when Linda and Bob climbed back to the ledge.

"Thanks for taking such good care of Gypsy last night," Kelly said as she stroked the dog's head.

Linda looked at her in surprise. "How'd you—" Linda stopped, then nodded her head knowingly. "So *you* were the midnight prowler!"

Kelly shrugged sheepishly. "Yes. I followed you and your friend back to the ranch the day you found Gypsy. I was hoping you'd take him home with you. I'd run out of dog food, and then he cut his foot, and I didn't have anything to put on it." She looked sadly at the little brown and white dog. He whined and licked her hand.

"But that night I got so lonely without him. I thought maybe if I could find some food for him, I could take Gypsy back."

"Peanut butter?" Linda said with a laugh.

Kelly nodded. "It's our favorite! But when I dropped the jar, I panicked and ran."

"What are you doing up here, anyway?" Bob asked. "It's not the best place for a vacation."

For a second Kelly didn't answer. "If I tell you, do you promise not to say anything to anyone?" She looked at them pleadingly.

"I don't know." Linda glanced at Bob. "It depends." She bent down in front of Kelly and began to wrap the bandage around her swollen ankle.

"On what?" The other girl winced in pain.

"On what you tell us," Bob answered.

Kelly dropped her eyes to the ground. "I ran away," she said in a quiet voice.

"Ran away!" Linda gasped. "Why?"

"Because my parents were going to sell Cinder." Kelly's voice trembled, and her eyes filled with tears. "My stepfather lost his job, and he said we couldn't afford to keep her anymore."

"Couldn't *you* have found a part-time job?" Linda asked.

"I thought about that," Kelly said, wiping a tear from her cheek. "But then they told me we had to move into town. They had found an apartment in Lockwood. There was no way I could earn enough money to board Cinder at a ranch."

Linda secured the bandage with a pin and sat back on her heels. Kelly was sobbing openly now.

"I guess running away was kind of dumb," she said between sobs. "But I didn't know what else to do."

"I know how you feel." Linda put a comforting hand on Kelly's shoulder. "I could never give up Amber."

She closed her first-aid kit and stood up. Then, once Kelly had stopped crying, Bob stepped over, and together they helped the injured girl to her feet.

"Don't put any weight on it," Bob cautioned. "It might be broken."

With Bob on one side of Kelly and Linda on the other, they started down the bank of rock to where the horses waited.

"You know, you really had the town in an uproar," Linda told her.

"What are you talking about?" Kelly asked nervously.

"Ghosts!" Bob chuckled. "My sister thought she was seeing the mysterious Ghost Horse."

"I *knew* it was a real horse," Linda retorted. "I just couldn't prove it!"

"Ghosts?" Kelly echoed in a puzzled voice. Linda told her Mac's tale and everything that had happened over the last few days.

When they reached Amber, Kelly steadied herself on the stirrup while Bob went to get Cinder and Rocket.

"I hope you're not mad at me for breaking into your house," she said anxiously. "I wasn't going to take anything except the peanut butter."

"I know that," Linda replied, and the girl seemed to relax. "But there is something I'm curious about," Linda added in a low voice. "How come I couldn't find any of Cinder's hoofprints? And how come your horse acts like she's part mountain goat? And how come when I saw your horse, it always looked like she had no rider?"

Kelly laughed at Linda's questions. "Cinder's a mustang. I bought her when she was just a yearling. In a way, her type of horse *is* part mountain goat!

"Because her hooves are so tough, I don't have

to shoe her, so she doesn't make much of a track in hard ground."

"Where did you learn to ride so well?" Linda asked.

"My stepfather taught me." Kelly smiled. "He used to be a trick-rider with the rodeo."

Linda's eyes lit up. "Really!"

"He wouldn't let me use a saddle, and he taught me lots of tricks. Like how to slip sideways when a horse is running, so no one can see you."

"Maybe you can show me how to do that!" Linda said excitedly. "It might come in handy when I'm trying to play a trick on my brother's friend Larry."

Just then, Bob came up, leading Rocket and Cinder. The black horse nickered softly when she saw her owner. Kelly, grabbing Cinder's long mane, hopped over to her. Seeing Cinder nuzzle Kelly's hand, Linda could tell how much the two meant to each other.

"Let me give you a boost up," Bob offered. "Then we'll get your things from the cave. You've got to get that ankle x-rayed."

A look of fear crossed Kelly's face. "No!" She spun around on one leg. "My ankle will be fine."

Bob looked at her wide-eyed. "Come on, Kelly. Get serious!"

"I can't go to a doctor," she insisted.

Linda had an idea of what the other girl was afraid of.

"Don't worry," she said. "My grandparents will help you figure out a way to keep Cinder."

Still Kelly didn't move.

"What if they can't?" she said, trembling.

"Trust me." Linda smiled. "They'll think of something."

Reluctantly, Kelly hopped to her horse's left side. Bob cupped his hands under the blond girl's bent knee.

"One, two, three!" he said, and lifted her into the air.

Light as a feather, Kelly swung her leg over Cinder's rump and settled onto the mare's back.

"Let's lead the horses to the stream," Bob suggested. "We don't want any more accidents."

Linda agreed. After watching her horse almost topple down the mountainside, she was ready to take it easy.

When they reached the cave, Bob and Linda crawled inside to retrieve Kelly's gear. Again, the little dog led the way. He barked gleefully, as if happy to have all his friends with him.

Inside the small cavern off the main chamber, Bob tied Kelly's sleeping bag to her knapsack and hoisted the bundle onto his back.

"Here. Take the flashlight. Check that I got everything," he told Linda. "I can find my way out."

Linda shone the light around the cave floor. Then she kicked the fire, making sure there were no remaining sparks. As she brushed the toe of her boot through the charred wood, a gleam caught her eye.

Using a stick, she dug through the wood until she spotted a piece of metal. She picked up the object and shone the flashlight on it. It was a heart-shaped locket, the kind that goes on a chain.

Wiping the locket on her jeans, she cleaned off the black soot. When it was clean, Linda saw that the locket was made of gold. For a moment, she thought it must be Kelly's. But when she looked closer, she realized the locket was dented and worn, as if it had been in the cave a long time.

Wondering whose it could be, she flipped the locket over, and the blood rushed from her face.

Engraved on the back, in fancy letters, was the name *Rachel!*

Linda blinked in surprise at the gold locket. Holding the flashlight closer, she read the name again—*Rachel.*

Could it have belonged to Rachel Manlon?

Bursting with excitement, Linda hurried out of the cave.

"Bob! Look what I found!" She waved the flashlight in the air to get his attention. He was tying Kelly's gear to his saddle.

"What?" he asked without looking up.

"A locket with Rachel Manlon's name on it!"

Bob stopped what he was doing and stared at her with interest. "You're sure?"

Linda dropped the piece of jewelry into his outstretched hand.

He held it carefully between his fingers and studied the inscription. "All it says is 'Rachel.' How do you know it's Rachel Manlon's?"

"Let me see." Kelly steered Cinder next to Bob and leaned over.

"I was making sure the fire was dead, when I saw it in the ashes," Linda told her. "It might belong to the girl in the story about the Ghost Horse."

"You mean I've been sleeping in a cave with a ghost?" Kelly cried, her mouth falling open.

Bob laughed at the expression on her face. "I wouldn't worry," he said. "My sister gets a little carried away. I doubt that the locket was Rachel Manlon's. That was twenty years ago!"

Linda snatched the locket from his hand and stuck it in her jeans pocket.

"If you're such a know-it-all, then whose is it?" she demanded.

Bob checked to make sure the bundle of gear was secure, then mounted Rocket. "Maybe it belonged to some Girl Scout working on her nature badge," he teased, and, reining the bay in a half-circle, he started for the old miner's trail. Wagging his tail, Gypsy ran beside Rocket.

"Brothers," Linda muttered.

"I know what you mean. I've got two of them," Kelly said. "And they always think they know everything!"

Linda gathered up her reins and mounted Amber. When they reached the miner's trail, Bob was waiting for them. Linda jumped off the palomino and lifted Gypsy into Kelly's arms.

For about a mile, they rode in silence. Then Kelly turned toward Linda, a puzzled frown creasing her brow.

"You know," the blond girl said. "Now that I think about it, the whole time I was living in the cave, I kept worrying about Cinder and how I was going to get food. But I was never really afraid of being alone. Even on the spookiest nights, I felt like someone was watching over me—though I knew there was no one there."

Linda stared at her, and goose bumps prickled up her arm. Then Kelly sighed and started talking about losing Cinder, and Linda wasn't sure if the other girl had been serious or not.

When they were almost to the ranch, Linda saw two riders in the distance. They were jogging toward them across the grasslands.

"It's Bronco and Doña," Bob said over his shoulder.

"Our grandparents," Linda explained to Kelly. She squeezed her heels against Amber's sides and cantered forward to meet them.

Kelly, not sure what kind of greeting she would get, hung back.

"Hello!" Bronco called out. He was mounted on his stallion, Colonel.

Doña, riding the ranch's Paso Fino stallion, El Capitán, to exercise him, nodded hello. Then she trotted the spirited gray in a circle, trying to calm him.

"We were hoping to meet up with you," Bronco said. Then he looked directly at Kelly. "You must be Kelly Michaels."

"How'd you know?" Linda blurted out.

"We phoned the police this morning to report the break-in," Doña explained.

Kelly's face went white. "They're not going to arrest me!"

"Of course not!" Bronco chuckled. "The sheriff just told us about a girl who ran away on a black horse five days ago. We figured whoever it was must be riding Linda's Ghost Horse."

"Kelly's been living in a cave on Coyote Mountain." Linda told them everything, except the part about Kelly confessing she was the prowler.

"Honey, your parents must be worried sick," Doña said to the blond girl. "You should call and tell them you're okay."

Kelly hung her head. "I can't call them," she protested.

"I don't understand." Doña looked confused. "Why not?"

Kelly looked at Doña and Bronco. There were tears in her eyes. "Because they're the reason I ran away. They want to sell Cinder." She leaned forward to hug her horse's neck.

For an awkward moment, no one said anything. Then Linda cleared her throat. "I told her you'd help her."

Bronco tipped back his cowboy hat. "We'll do everything we can," he promised. "But it's still up to Kelly and her parents."

"Right now, Kelly needs her ankle x-rayed." Bob spoke up for the first time. "It might be broken."

"Why didn't you say so?" Doña exclaimed, letting El Capitán break into a canter. "We're wasting time standing here!"

When they arrived at the ranch, Doña and Bronco handed their horses over to Bob. Linda took charge of Cinder and the dog, Gypsy.

"I'll take good care of them while you're at the clinic," Linda promised as her grandparents helped Kelly climb into the jeep. She waved goodbye, then clucked to the two horses and led them into the barn. Gypsy followed the horse.

With a pat of apology, Linda cross-tied Amber in the aisle, snapping the two ropes on either side of her bit.

"You'll just have to be patient while I feed Cinder," Linda told the palomino.

Finding an empty stall, she led the black mare in and unbridled her. When she had poured a measure of grain into the feed tub, Cinder attacked it greedily. Then Linda went to unsaddle Amber.

"Sorry to make you wait," she said, digging in her pocket for a carrot.

As she did, her fingers brushed against something smooth—the gold locket. She'd forgotten all about it!

She pulled the heart-shaped pendant out of her pocket and stared at it. Is there any way to prove it *was* Rachel Manlon's? she wondered. Would Rachel's brother, Glen, know?

She didn't really want to ask him. Not after the way he'd behaved in Lockwood. But she had to have an answer.

"Bob! Will you take Kelly's dog and feed him when you go in?" she called as she stuck the locket back in her jeans pocket.

"Sure. Where're you going?"

"I've got an errand to run. Tell Luisa I'll be late for dinner."

Linda unsnapped the cross ties and led Amber from the barn. Already the sun was beginning to set, casting a pink glow on the trees. But the Manlon ranch was only a couple of miles past Rancho del Sol, and if she took a shortcut, she could be there before dark. She mounted Amber and urged her forward.

A few minutes later, Linda began to have second thoughts. Was she doing the right thing?

She was about to turn back, when she caught sight of a cluster of buildings around a bend.

"I've come this far," she said to herself. "I'm not turning back now!" She urged Amber forward and turned left into Manlon's drive.

As Amber jogged up the dusty lane, Linda noticed how run-down the barns were. Then she saw the house, and her heart skipped a beat.

It looked dark and gloomy against the pink sky, and the windows were all closed as if no one was home.

Suddenly, a shutter slapped in the wind, and Amber skittered sideways. Nervously, Linda tightened her hold, slowing the mare to a walk as they approached the house. Then Linda saw Manlon's jeep parked around the corner.

Might as well get it over with, she told herself, though her heart was still thumping wildly.

She dismounted and led Amber to the front of the house. The mare eyed the sagging porch as if it were a monster.

"Easy, girl," Linda soothed, wrapping the reins around the railing.

Then, taking a deep breath, she climbed the rickety stairs and knocked on the door.

No one answered.

With a sigh of relief, Linda turned to go. Just then, the door creaked open, and Glen Manlon stepped onto the porch.

Too surprised to say anything, Linda just stared.

The man before her was tall, even taller than she remembered, and had deep shadows beneath his eyes. His hair was rumpled, and there was no smile of greeting on his face.

"Can I help you?" he asked quietly, though his grim expression didn't change.

"Uh, yes," Linda stammered. "My name's Linda Craig, and my brother and I were up on Coyote Mountain, and we found this." She held out the locket.

Without a word, he reached out and took it from her hand. Then he read the inscription, and his face turned red.

"Is this your idea of a joke?" he growled.

Startled by his reaction, Linda stepped backward, bumping into the porch railing.

"No! I thought it might be your sister's!" she explained hastily.

"My sister's!" Manlon laughed hoarsely. "How could it belong to her? Rachel has been gone twenty years."

He tossed the locket over the porch railing. "That's what I think of your joke. Now get off my ranch, and don't ever come back!"

Linda didn't hesitate. She turned and clattered

down the porch steps. She scrambled into the saddle and dug her heels into Amber's sides. The mare took off, her hooves pounding in the dirt as they galloped down the drive.

Coming here had been a mistake, and all Linda wanted now was to get as far away from this place as possible.

She held tightly to the mare's mane, letting Amber have her head. They were almost to the trail when Linda heard the roar of a jeep.

He was coming after them!

At the bend in the drive, Linda tried to steer the palomino to the left. But Amber resisted the command. Shortening her grip on the reins, Linda tugged again, forcing her horse in the direction Linda wanted to take.

Reluctantly, Amber cantered down the trail until they came to a woods. The sun was setting, and the woods were dark with shadows. Linda slowed the mare, afraid she would step into a hole.

Then Linda saw lights up ahead. Was Manlon still following them?

She decided to take a risk and pushed the palomino into a gallop. A moment later, Amber bounded out of the woods right onto a two-lane highway.

A car whizzed past.

Startled, the mare spun around, her metal horseshoes skidding on the slick pavement. She was starting to fall, when Linda looked up and saw a tractor-trailer heading straight for them!

10 ♦♦♦♦

As the huge truck bore down on them, Linda jerked the reins so hard that Amber reared backward. But the split-second move saved their lives.

Twisting her body sideways, Amber leapt to the side of the road. The sudden jolt unseated Linda, and she flew into the air, landing on her back in the grass.

With a honk of its horn, the tractor-trailer roared past.

Linda gasped for breath. At the same time, she could hear Amber snorting next to her.

"Amber!" she called, and when the mare lowered her head to snuffle her cheek, Linda grabbed the dangling reins. She didn't want the palomino wandering back onto the road.

"I'm okay," Linda wheezed. At least she thought she was. But for the moment, she knew she'd better lie quietly and catch her breath.

Then she heard the squeal of brakes and the sound of a door slamming. Someone was stopping.

Footsteps thudded on the pavement, then rustled in the grass. A moment later, a shadowy face leaned over her.

It was Glen Manlon!

"Are you all right?" he asked anxiously.

Linda stared at him suspiciously. What was he doing there? Why had he followed her? Unable to run, she felt helpless. A momentary feeling of panic washed over her.

"Look, I'm sorry if I scared you before," Manlon said, seeing the nervous expression on Linda's face. "I didn't mean to." He knelt down beside her.

Linda propped herself up on her elbows.

"Is that why you were following me?" she asked, looking him boldly in the eyes. She was trying to pretend she wasn't afraid. "To apologize?"

"Yes. I behaved badly at the ranch. Are you okay?" he asked, still worried.

She nodded.

"Anything broken?"

Gingerly, Linda wiggled her toes, then lifted her arms and legs.

"No," she reported. "I just had the wind knocked out of me."

"Thank goodness you're all right. You scared the daylights out of me when you charged down the path to the highway."

"It was my fault." Linda sat all the way up. "Amber tried to tell me it was the wrong trail. But it was getting dark, and I was scared . . ."

"No, it was *my* fault," Manlon interrupted. "When you took off, I realized how gruff I must've sounded."

Then he smiled, and the hard lines in his face softened.

Linda smiled back, thinking he wasn't so bad after all. He held out his hand and helped her to her feet.

"My legs are a little wobbly, but other than that, I'm fine," she said when she stood up.

"Let me drive you home."

"No. I'd rather ride."

"Then I'll follow alongside in the jeep."

Linda accepted his offer. It was too dark to ride

back on the trail, and the traffic on the road was heavier than usual.

He boosted her into the saddle, then jogged over to his jeep. The lights of the vehicle illuminated a clear path down the side of the highway, and Linda was glad he had offered to follow her home.

When they reached Rancho del Sol, Bronco and Doña hurried from the house, Bob right behind them.

"Are you okay?" Bronco asked. His voice was gruff, which meant he'd been worried.

Doña caught the side of Amber's bridle while Linda dismounted. "We were afraid something had happened to you!"

"No. I'm fine."

Without opening the door, Glen Manlon vaulted out of the jeep. "Something almost did happen!"

Bronco and Doña gave their granddaughter a questioning look.

"It's a long story," Linda said, not wanting to explain the situation right then.

"I'll put Amber in her stall," Bob offered.

Reluctantly, Linda handed him the reins. It was her job to care for Amber, especially after all the mare had done. But she was suddenly feeling very tired. It had been a long day!

Bob led Amber to the barn.

"We saved some dinner for you," Doña said. Then she invited Glen Manlon in for coffee and dessert.

Wearily, Linda followed the adults. Then she remembered the locket, and she began to hurry. Maybe Manlon would tell them about Rachel. He seemed more relaxed now.

"How does homemade blueberry pie sound?" Bronco was saying to Glen Manlon as he ushered the younger man into the dining room.

Linda followed Doña into the kitchen. Wearing hot mitts, her grandmother pulled a plate of food from the oven.

"How's Kelly's ankle, Doña?" Linda asked.

"Fine," Doña replied. "It's just sprained. Right now she's in Bronco's office with her leg propped up. We had a long talk on the way to the clinic."

"Did she call her parents?" Linda wanted to know.

"Not yet, but we set the phone by the chair, hoping she'll call them soon."

Doña placed the plate and a glass of milk on a tray and carried it to the dining room.

"As soon as I eat, I'll go and visit with Kelly," Linda said.

"That's a good idea," Doña said as she returned to the kitchen for the coffee and pie.

Bronco and Glen Manlon were sitting at the table, talking. As Linda sat down, she listened closely. But they were only discussing the price of cattle.

When Doña arrived with dessert and the coffee pot, Bronco turned to his granddaughter. "Now, let's hear this lo-o-ong story," he said.

Linda swallowed a bite of steak, and was about to speak, when Manlon started talking.

"I think I should do the explaining," he told the Mallorys. "Your granddaughter very kindly brought me this locket." He drew it from his shirt pocket and laid it on the table. "In return, I scared her so badly, she almost got hit by a truck!"

"It wasn't *all* your fault," Linda protested.

"Most of it was my fault. All week long people in town have been badgering me about the Ghost Horse. I even drove into the mountains to see if there was any truth to what they were saying. I didn't find anything. So when you handed me the locket, I thought it was just another prank."

"I should have realized—"

Manlon cut Linda off with a wave of his hand. "When I looked closer at the locket," he continued, "I saw it was the same one I'd given Rachel for her sixteenth birthday. Right before she ran away."

Linda almost dropped her fork. "It really is?"

"Yes." He stared down at his coffee cup. Silently, Doña served him a piece of pie. He nodded a thank-you, then looked up. Abruptly, he straightened in his chair and stared at the doorway.

Kelly was standing in the dining-room doorway, a crutch under one arm. The little dog, Gypsy, was beside her.

Across the table from Linda, Glen Manlon let out his breath.

"For a second there, you looked just like my sister," he said, shaking his head. But his grin showed relief.

"That's Kelly," Linda explained. "She's the reason everyone was asking you about the Ghost Horse."

"Linda!" Doña admonished gently. "Finish your dinner."

"Did you call your folks?" Bronco asked the blond girl.

Kelly nodded yes and slid into a chair. Doña cut her a slice of pie.

"You were right. They were really glad to hear from me. We had a long talk, and . . ." Her voice began to quiver. "They understand a little better how I feel about selling Cinder. They just don't know how they can afford not to."

Kelly's eyes began to fill with tears. Linda felt terrible for her.

"Would somebody mind telling me what's going on?" Manlon asked.

"I'm sure Linda would love to." Bronco chuckled.

Between bites of pie, Linda and Kelly explained all about Kelly's reasons for running away. When they had finished, Glen Manlon shook his head.

"I understand all too well," he told Kelly. "Twenty years ago, I told my sister, Rachel, that I had to sell her horse, Glimmer.

"It had been a tough year. Our parents had died,

and then we lost half our livestock in the spring floods."

He frowned to himself, remembering the hard times. "To me the most important thing was keeping the ranch going—even if it meant selling Glimmer. She was the best we had, and I had lots of interested buyers. The money would've bought a couple of new cattle.

"But to Rachel, the most important thing was her horse. I just didn't listen when she told me." He looked up, and the grim expression was once again on his face. "So she ran away. And there isn't a day that goes by when I don't wonder where she is." He stared directly at Kelly. "Don't make your parents suffer as I have."

Speechless, Kelly nodded. Even Linda had a lump in her throat.

Then Glen Manlon smiled and said heartily, "Now, I'd say we've got some work to do."

"We do?" Kelly asked.

"Sure. We have to figure out a way for you to keep Cinder!"

Kelly's eyes lit up. "You mean you'll help?" she asked hopefully.

"You bet I will," Manlon said, nodding.

"I know!" Linda looked at him pointedly. "*Somebody* could give Kelly a part-time job at his ranch! I mean, she isn't moving all that far, and you should see her ride!"

"I could work one or two days after school and on weekends," Kelly chimed in.

"Sounds good to me. Now, I wonder who would hire you?" Glen Manlon said, scratching his chin as he pretended to think it over.

While the two girls stared at him expectantly, Bronco and Doña started to laugh.

"Let's see." Manlon's mouth slid into a grin. "I might be able to use somebody around the place. Only I can't afford to pay much, Kelly," he added quickly. "So how about if you work for all the hay and grain Cinder can eat?"

"You mean it?" Kelly jumped up and hopped over to him. "Thank you!" She shook his hand seriously, then whooped like a little kid.

"Well, I'm glad that's solved!" Bob chuckled. "Now I can finish my pie!"

"How about another piece?" Doña asked everyone.

"Not for me," Linda replied. "I need to check on Amber."

She grabbed an apple from the centerpiece and headed for the kitchen door. As she walked slowly across the lawn, she thought about all the neat things that had happened. Now Kelly could keep her horse, and Glen Manlon would have some company!

Suddenly, she heard Amber neigh loudly from the pasture. Figuring Bob had forgotten to feed her, Linda broke into a jog. She stopped in the barn to grab a lead rope, then went out back.

Amber was standing in the middle of the corral, looking toward Coyote Mountain. Linda rested her arms on the top railing and gazed across the mesa.

The moon was rising over the top of the mountain, and, just like on the night they'd camped out, it cast a blue glow over the countryside.

Linda smiled, remembering how Mac's tale had scared them and how, later, she'd started to believe there really *was* a ghost!

And to think it had only been Kelly and Cinder!

With a chuckle, Linda opened the corral gate and whistled.

But Amber didn't move. She stood as still as a statue—her neck arched, her nose pointed toward the mountain.

Linda followed Amber's gaze. Then, with a jolt of surprise, she realized what the mare was staring at so intently.

Silhouetted against the moon, the black shape of a horse and rider galloped across the jagged ridge.

Or was it just a cloud?